o

*******Touching, incisive, tr**
Funny, touching, incisive and ....easure...
Coombe deals deftly with difficult subjects… The writing is
efficient, sharp and entertaining; with a wry, self-deprecating
wit that keeps it clear of self-pity. The ideal handbook for
seekers everywhere. (Baileyology. Twitter. Amazon)

*******Cyrano de Bergerac meets Bridget Jones**, 9 Sep 2011
At times fast, furious, shocking even, the language colourful,
painting vivid pictures from beginning to end. (Antonella.
Amazon)

*******Compassionate, funny, well-written**, 30 Aug 2011
Orange … grabs you right from the first sentence… Cherry
Coombe tells the story from the standpoint of one who has
been through it and seen the harm which can be suffered by
the idealist at the hands of the exploitative, the selfish or the
plain stupid, but she tells it with compassion and with the
understanding of age and experience… Honest, funny, tragic,
intelligent, perspicacious and above all well-written, Orange is
an engaging story which will broaden the understanding of
anyone who reads it, and will engage and entertain them as it
does so. (R.B. Amazon)

*******Hippy Trip!**, 25 Aug 2011
The story-telling is refreshingly honest and the plot at times is
quite tragic, while the author's brilliant irony makes many of
the episodes 'laugh out loud' funny. (C.J. Randell Amazon)

New reviews and news at: www.cherrycoombe.com

ORANGE

Cherry Coombe

www.cherrycoombe.com

Rosie's absurdly disturbing story rampages between Oxfordshire, India and Sao Paulo as her search for enlightenment exposes the dark underbelly of 70s peace and love. As she lampoons her own unresolved relationships, interwoven stories unravel and the past intrudes on the present. Fragments of experience shared; fish-stew, joints and 70s sex; mistaken identity and coincidence colour a kaleidoscope of intersecting lives. Unfinished business agitates and craves an end, propelling a passionate story of life and love across four decades.

Madge –
I hope this doesn't
make your ears hurt!
All Love.

ORANGE

[signature]

10·12·11.

Cherry Coombe

To Bonny and Rowan, with love

ACKNOWLEDGEMENTS

Many people have supported the development of this novel. I am particularly indebted to Claire Soni and Bonny Coombe for reading and commenting on the text.

The locations of events in this novel are the usual mix of the real and the imaginary. Characters are drawn as an amalgam of stereotypes prevalent through distinct decades; they and their actions are entirely fictitious creations drawn from a range of prolific motifs of their era, with a possible exception in the depiction of the master or 'Bhagwan' of the Pune ashram, inspired in particular by Osho Rajneesh who is now celebrated by many. Any other similarity to real persons, dead or alive, is coincidental and not intended by the author.

Cherry Coombe
www.cherrycoombe.com

BUCKINGHAMSHIRE, 2003

An old friend, Premda, came to visit in the spring of 2003. I hadn't seen him for 22 years. Premda was in Australia for so long that his father died and his daughter grew up without his noticing. His full name is Swami Anand Premda, which means 'the bringer and sharer of love' although he is English and his mother christened him Derek. I went to meet Premda at Heathrow at 5.20am. Premda was very sexy in 1981. Two children of my own and several steps, grey hair and a skin condition made famous by Michael Jackson made it impossible to leave the house without makeup. I got up before I went to bed. I visited the Ladies in Terminal 4 five times to check I didn't have lipstick on my teeth and that I didn't smell of fags. I'd decided I'd leap the barrier when I spotted Premda and sucker my lips to his neck. I anticipated a bit of a tussle with the baggage trolley but that was all. The electricity mounting between me and the man with a sign saying 'BT Openworld WILLIAM'S' reassured me. He smiled more broadly on each of my trips to the Ladies.

A number of men with brown knees and tired eyes shivered through the barricade and my mouth dried. When the moment came I forgot the barrier vaulting. I peered and he peered and I drooled over his sleek Gladstone bag, the brogues, the svelte Mills and Boon greying temples. He beamed at my left shoulder and The Lady in Red behind me. The eyebrows were wrong. The next was swathed in stretchy T-shirt material, a vest with an unbuttoned hoody; ponytail, grey; beard, grey; and some bags: grey and safer because of the string. I thought, 'I hope to God that's not him'. He looked back at me as he got to the end of the line and I thought, 'Shit, damn, bugger-me, it is. Fuck, it's him.'

"Oh. Hello darling. It is you. I thought. We looked. And it is you. Wow. Mmm," he said.

Once I'd driven Premda round the M25, up the M1 and back to my house the shops were just about to open. He and I walked down the road into the village to get some bacon and we'd been in the shop for 30 seconds when he started toning: aum-ing and chanting with mustard-jar-shattering intensity. Robbins for Everything. 8.30. Monday morning. In a very small town. Where I live.

When we got back to my house, my son, Rob, was tucking his sandwiches into his Adidas bag with his books. He and Premda shook hands.

Guinea Pig Television had come up with a new idea. It was called *My New Best Friend* and it required a volunteer to let a complete stranger turn up on their door-step and pretend to be their lost best friend of 20 summers past. If the volunteer got through two days of ordinary life in the company of the phoney friend, without revealing to friends and family that they'd been scammed, they won £1,000 from Channel Four. Perhaps rates payable were reasonable for an embarrassing geezer to play the part of the new best friend: a scruffy hippy that did a lot of old-age new-age stuff in inappropriate places.

The handshake was enough for Rob but Premda added,

"Hi Rob. You're beautiful." My son dragged me outside, around the corner of the house and threatened to leave.

"If you're on that TV show, and you think you can get away with this, you can fuck off." I had to commiserate and laugh with him about how weird the whole thing was and give him a fiver before he'd believe me. TV might have hurt less.

I decided to reunite friends from 1974 and hold a party at my house. When I'd last seen many of these people we were all leaving the ashram, Pune, India. Some went to Oregon with the absconding master to gain notoriety for improving the world, but later, for atrocities carried out in the name of love. Premda, last seen, had been in a long orange robe and was going to America to the Oregon commune, but I had reverted to corduroy trousers in a tight fit on my return to England. While I had become engrossed in everyday life in an ordinary sort of way - polo necks, two children, step-children, terraced house, divorce and so on - Premda had travelled with Shamans, tested and modified Ecstasy and lived with the Dalai Lama's monks. Most of us wondered how we had become enslaved by life-styles for cars no better than Premda's. We hugged and talked about enlightenment at the reunion party. Premda deduced that we had all been shopping in the same supermarket but had been on different aisles. Seduced by the idea, I relegated marriage to aisle 7 not far from Tantra in aisle 5. Same hymn book, different hymn.

Freya, my daughter, scoffed "grow-up" while we talked of how we had.

1972–1976

Nothing much happened in Streatley-on-Thames. There was a youth hostel and a succession of envious trekkers in thick socks, preparing for or recovering from the ascent to Aldworth where the Ridgeway peaked and red kites circled as if to gloat. They came and went. There was a bit of excitement when Danny La Rue took over the Swan Hotel and covered it in fairy lights but the Residents' Association soon put a stop to that. Areas of outstanding natural beauty won't tolerate the garish.

Just two events stood out in adolescence. Everyone has at least one serious crush. The subject of my own was an impoverished Irish artist, Patrick Connor, at least eight or nine years my senior, who I knew took gardening jobs between commissions. He was made especially attractive by living in the gatehouse to a cemetery and for holding wild parties beneath a makeshift gazebo strung between two of the taller memorials. My bedroom, at a good safe five-mile distance from the cemetery, looked over instead the knee of the Berkshire Downs as they bent their way to stand in the Thames below, the river dividing them from the Chilterns.

Wrapped round the back of my family's home were the rolling gardens carved by the rich from National Trust property, and so nature posed problems to stock-brokers, exhausted from hard days' trading. Such territory suggested no threat to Patrick Connor, however, used as he was to uncovering immense brass sculptures from heavy clay moulds. Only a fence separated me, Rosie Taylor, from the man of my waking meditations as he cleared the orchard next-door, where my father piled compost beyond his careful bonfire. Between my first and second A level years, nestled in the hot, sweet mulch of composting leaves, Patrick introduced me to love, and never let it be said the first is not the best. But that was a one-off.

The other memorable interlude lasted a day and a night and started when I was baby-sitting for several of the seven children born to the couple who owned the famous village cheese shop. It was a drizzly day and, for eight hours, I had been fascinated by the two punks failing to hitch a lift at the crossroads. As I returned home to an empty house, my own parents having taken off for Europe with the tent, again, I invited the two home for a warm. These two, Tim and Katherine, were wanted by the police but that was no concern of mine.

Tim and Katherine had very little: some Speed, which I declined, and their love, but I was struck by their determination to escape. They explained they had come from very tough homes and that their love was disallowed. After some pork chops and a bottle of my father's wine, I made them a cosy bed between two sofas pushed together and suggested they tried the bus the next day in preference to hitching. But when I got up they'd gone, and they'd taken £5 from my purse. I was more hurt than angry because I had nothing to do once they'd gone. So I caught the bus to Reading to see if I could find them, but of course I never did. A few weeks later the local newspaper ran the headline, 'Runaway Northampton School-girl Dies in Reading' which I thought might solve the mystery, but this girl was a Lesley and the one I'd met was called Katherine. This too was soon annexed to 'fun I nearly had' and my search for a new group of friends had to start again.

School was less picturesque than home and even less happened there, although the legendary art teacher, Ron Freeborn, had his A level 'all girls' out in all weathers trying to capture the curves of Didcot Power Station in the changing light. We suffered a sexual desert through several summers of 70s love. I was nothing if not resourceful.

I'd teamed up in the art-block with Fiona Cave who was rumoured to be dating Ron and was always immaculately turned out. We were an odd pair: me in cheesecloth and Wranglers, Fiona in court shoes and polyester, but needs must. Fiona's friend, Roger, ran Ballroom Dancing classes at the local psychiatric hospital and she took me along for the ride. Crowds of the sedated insane schmoozed with same-sex blobs, drooling over the flip-down selection of 45s stacked under the arm of the gramophone. There's always a price.

Fairmile was a brick-built Victorian asylum; a teaching psychiatric hospital that had commandeered three manor houses stretched along the A4329 to house its student nurses. Bob Moore, long-haired cockney with an A30 he'd bought for 30 bob and Derek Lawson, ex-marine with one tattoo, came along to ballroom dancing to see if they could pull. I was changing the record.

"Hi." They smiled in unison.

"Hello. Um. Are you, um? Have you got your ward numbers?" They liked that. Gave each other the look and homed in. Derek began,

"What's a nice girl like you doing in a place like this?" but Bob was hot on his heels.

"Don't take any notice of that tosser, love. Look, you don't want to be hanging around here on a Tuesday do you? Really? Can you dance?"

"Well, not like this, you know. I'm more of a Pink Floyd fan at heart."

Derek massaged an ego still wet behind the ears.

"Of course you are. You're one of us."

"Charmer. Derek, look, give the girl a break. Go easy on her son. What's your name?"

"Rosie. Yours?"

"Bob. Also known as the Arts Director extraordinaire."

"I like Art. I'm doing it for A level."

"Didcot Girls'?"

"Yeah. How did you know?"

"I've been here long enough to spot one of the Grammar lot. Been to a few of their shows. Weren't you in that Ron's production of The Crucible?" I blushed. He was right but I'd had to play Giles and had modelled my part on my grandfather. I didn't think that was how I wanted Bob to see me.

"Well. Yes I was. What are you going to girls' school plays for, for Christ sake? I spend my life trying to get out of that place." I blushed some more.

"Pantomime. I wanted to look at the lighting."

"I'm the Dame," said Derek.

"Yeah, alright. Keep yer hair on Dek. Gi'us a chance here. Look. We've got a bit of a Snow White problem."

"You're the pantomime producer? Wow." I blushed some more. Fiona, super cool, came over and changed the record. Someone was having a grand mal and the charge nurse had put all the lights on full.

7

"Last dance ladies and gentlemen," said Fiona, tapping her pink fingernails on the melamine tabletop.

"Oh, sorry Fiona. It's just, um, we were just talking about"

"The pantomime," said Bob. "We need a new Snow White."

"You carry on sweetie. I know you'd rather think about, um, the pantomime did you say, than this lot? Roger and I'll pack up and perhaps this young man,"

"Bob. Student nurse."

"Thank you Bob. Perhaps you'll walk Rosie to her bus will you? Good chap." Fiona released me.

It was all downhill from there. I gave up Largactil infested pirouettes and started hanging out with Bob and Derek. Snow White and Some Dwarfs saved my life. We'd gather at least three times a week for Bob to hurl abuse,

"What you got? Shit for brains? Rocks in yer head? I said stage left not fucking right" and it was all a refreshing change from Ron.

After rehearsals there was Lowenbrau on tap in the hospital social club and a stagger along the A4329 to Moulsford Manor and Bob and Derek's attic rooms: guitars, joints and more than seven dwarfs hitting on me, one by one. The 70s took off.

1972–1976

II

The pantomime filled my last three terms at school. We couldn't get it on stage by Christmas. The patients, our audience, wore shorts and Santa Claus hats, becoming confused and over-excited in flaming June. Images of Krishna and mandalas nearly ruined Ron Freeborn's reputation as a Fine Art teacher that year but he was sorry to let his girls go, and some shone on. I spent the summer in Wales, nearly flying with the hang-gliders from the cliffs at Rosilly but Derek and Bob held on to me until I came down. We lived in a tent on chocolate and bananas while I mastered a language my parents just didn't understand.

We had to go back.

I guess we'd only been away for a fortnight but memory does funny things to time. Bob and Derek had to get on with their training to become psychiatric nurses, and my parents thought I should get a job if I wanted a year out. Someone someone knew told me about a job in the Occupational Therapy department at Borough Court Hospital, Peppard

Common. There were really only hospitals and pubs in the country. I started working with the mentally subnormal, who came before language conveyed empathy. I had a room with a kiln and some paint and enough money to finance a Citroen 2CV, some Levis and a steady flow of Guinness and cider in the social club at lunchtime. In the evening I'd eat my mother's food and go out but things were starting to change.

Derek had gone rather strange. He'd given up dope but had gone all intense and huggy even without it. He got me on my own one night.

"Rosie, babe. I've got something for you." He passed me his bag.

"Look in there; I'm just going to get a couple of drinks in." I was relieved. I thought it was about time he harvested that grass he'd been growing in the eaves at Moulsford Manor. I couldn't believe he'd let it all go to waste; I'd even considered growing my own around my father's bonfire. There was a book, *The Prophet*: Kahil Gibran, but I'd seen that before, some candles and an envelope. I unzipped the pocket and he came back.

"The envelope, you silly cow. It's got your name on it."

I opened it. A glossy A4 brochure entitled, **Conquestadoor** *Humanistic Growth Centre*. I flicked through the pages and found something he'd circled:

48 Hour Encounter Marathon
with Gavin Machim
August 24-25
Arrive midnight August 23rd

Free yourself from the neurosis of your past. An intense experience of being fully alive to liberate you from the repression that dominates your choices. Learn how to relate freely and openly with others and discover that you are loveable in the safety and honesty of this group for twenty people.

£25. Send £20 payable to Gavin Machim to book your place. No refunds.

"How do you feel?"

"Well, to be honest with you, Derek, I think that I am loveable anyway and I'm not neurotic, if that's what you think. I thought you and I had something special, you know. Non-attached acceptance and love and everything. Who needs to, Christ, £25. That's what it cost for my afghan and my new boots. Anyway, I'm going to Reading Festival."

"I asked you how you feel. Not what you think. You're being very defensive."

I was shocked. I burst into tears.

"You're crying because you're angry. You've got so much anger in you that you're frightened to own."

"For fuck's sake, Derek." I tried to roll a fag but I'd only just learnt how to do that in Wales and I got tobacco embedded in the furry neck of my smelly coat.

"You don't value yourself, Rosie. Are you not worth as much as the clothes you wear?"

"Derek, what are you on about? You know I'm not

materialistic."

"Do you love me?"

"Yes, I love everybody."

"Right. Will you take a risk?"

"Of course I will. You know that. Look at Rosilly."

"Right. Trust me then and book up for this group."

"You're bloody mad, Dek. Will you come?"

"Just say yes, Rosie."

"As it's you, fuck it, eh? You only live this life once I suppose. Yeah alright."

Premda lent me the £25 until payday and Bob came along in his A30, which eventually expired and never left Kilburn again.

1972–1976

III

Gavin Machim, 31, Americanised-Glaswegian, scrawny, balding and pony tailed, wore faded Levis and a matching shirt. He came with: a Zippo lighter, 60 Players Navy Cut and his 'trainees', Mark Weatherby and Miah Roberts. Miah ticked off deposits and collected the rest while Mark checked addresses for mail-shots and took £2.75 extra for vegetarian food to be provided by Tim who we'd only see in the breaks.

At midnight, twenty of us sat in a circle. Cushions on stained green Axminster. The room, knocked through to extend from front to back of the North London terrace, was hot, sticky and tawdry. Buckets stood in four corners, the only other furniture a blackboard and two boxes of tissues. Inner hardboard window-shutters bowed against foam sandwiched between them and the glass.

Miah rang a bell.

"Midnight. Time. Quiet." It was already very quiet. "I'm Miah and I'll read the rules. I'd like anyone who feels they can't respect the rules to raise their hand. And, not now, thank you." A fat man in dungarees interrupted.

"It says in the brochure." Gavin was on his feet, flanked by Miah and Mark who were frowning and nodding.

"Shut the fuck up, motherfucker," roared Gavin. "Didn't your mummy ever tell you, you can't just have what the fuck you want whenever the fuck you wan it? Huh? Ring some bells does it, fat boy? Siddown and wait your turn like the rest of these fucked-up neurotics here. Miah." Gavin sat down. The fat man put a fruit pastille in his mouth and Miah carried on.

"Hands up for those with questions. The rules are: no eating, except when we send you for a food meditation; no leaving the room except when we tell you; if you need to pee, shit or throw up at any other time, use the buckets; no violence; no sex, drugs or alcohol and no leaving before the end of the experience. OK?" A woman in pink fluff with ironed jeans and full make up had her hand up. "Yes," said Miah. "Your question?"

"I don't think there's any need for Gavin to swear and to be insolent to someone he's never met before. Do you?" Miah wasn't having any of it.

"Listen, lady. I invited questions regarding the rules and I'm not interested in your hostile invitation for me to collude with your neurosis and deny you an experience of a new way of life here with Gavin." She was starting to shout now. Mark was pacing the ring on the outside. Miah went on, "Do you have a problem with the rules?"

"No. It's just that" Mark had just reached her space and yelled in her left ear,

"You can take your 'just that' and shove it up your arse. Have you got that?" The woman, who looked as if she already had enough up her arse, piped down and Miah nodded. Fat man stuck another fruit pastille in his mouth but not much got past Miah,

14

"I said no eating. Do you get that?" She held out a bucket in front of his cushion. He put his fruit pastilles in the bucket and the mousy man next to him pulled a small bottle of vodka out of his pocket and slipped that in too. Gavin got up. "Right. OK Miah, Mark. Thanks. Now. My name's Gavin. I'm the group leader, an ex addict, trained to run encounter groups with Vamoosh at The Last Chance Foundation. I know what's going on. You don't. Nobody challenges me. We're here to look at your dirty arses not mine. I don't give a fuck about what you think. I'm only interested in your feelings. By the way, I'm the only person that's going to be smoking in here. If you don't like it, you know what you can do. If you want to maintain your stuck position and resist me you can waste your £25 and break the rules. Do that and you leave. No refunds. If you want to go, go now." There was a pause. Bob, across from me and to Gavin's right, snarled. I put my finger across my mouth, terrified he was going to get a bollocking. Gavin stared at me and said scathingly,

"What's the matter, Daddy's little girl? Past your bedtime is it? Wanna go home?"

"No, I . . ."

"Yeah right. Hang it on the wall. You may all now go for a pee break. The group reconvenes at half past twelve, ten minutes from now. Leave your watches outside. We don't need any control freaks, right? There's a clock in the piss-house. Be ready to start, on time and no fucking around. Oh, yeah, and no talking on the break. OK?" There was a mad scramble for two toilets in a shrinking terraced house even though we'd only been there half an hour. I squeezed Bob's hand on the stairs but he didn't smile and I started to cry. The place stank of farting and Barley Cup. Nothing would flush and it felt like being in a war.

'Structures' divided the hours. At first we shared 'hidden

15

agendas' and Mark used the blackboard to illustrate a 'Jo-Hari' window which proved that if you told other people what you really thought and didn't avoid swearing they would be blessed with a glimpse of the x-factor which dominated their lives. Miah drew pictures of The Accepter, an oral and thus fat personality that would dash across the road of life without thinking of the consequences. The Rejecter looked like Gavin, I thought, and was anally retentive and so missed out on crossing the road at all. We were all there, I assumed, to learn the green cross code.

There was plenty of shouting and screaming and we all had image names. Mine stuck at 'Daddy's Little Girl', which hurt a lot since I thought I was a grown-up who'd been acting not being Snow White. Fatty was 'Angel Delight' and Mrs Pink was 'Syrup on Shit'. Bob was 'Jail Bird' which I thought was cool but he hated it because his mother was in prison. He and I became best friends with 'Donkey Dick' and 'Cling-on' after an eating meditation we did with them which meant feeding each other Tim's bananary yoghurty datey crunchy pudding while blindfolded.

There were male/female role reversals and master and slave games and times when we had to run round the room in circles screaming "get out of my way you cunt" at the person in front of us. It was lucky I'd spent the summer in Wales learning not to be middle-class. Only one person, a Brazilian woman called 'Wannabe', ahead of her time with pierced nipples, pissed in the bucket. She got it in the neck from Syrup on Shit who thought she should learn some decorum and who in turn got a rollicking from Donkey Dick who thought that Syrup should get over her fear of fellatio, right there and then. Luckily Angel Delight remembered the 'no sex' rule so Miah and Mark organised a synchronised 'trust your orgasm' exercise which involved getting Syrup to jump from the top of

16

a tall step-ladder into the arms of the group. I heard she later got-off with a man who specialised in ladders for Travis Perkins, West Hampstead.

Two days and no sleep later we spent the last two hours of the group in a synanon encounter circle, a technique derived from Freedom House Therapeutic Community for the heroin-addicted-personality, New York, and adapted to the needs of the Normal Healthy Neurotic owner-of-a-cheque-book, Hampstead. Naked, we made two firm fists and eye contact and when Mark said "go" we started screaming abuse at the person we faced. The racket ricocheted back into the room from the hardboard foam as we moved from face to face, encouraged by Mark and Gavin who prodded us from outside the circle with two foam batons (used earlier by a woman to thrash a cushion, representing her mother, to death).

"Get to everybody," encouraged Mark. "Don't sell yourself short."

"Really take a risk. All you've got to lose is your image," screamed Gavin. Miah, a junior trainee, had to join in but she said it was a privilege and a perk of the job. She told me I was a hostile, ice-cream-puke of a puppy-fatted, spotty child and I told her that her tits made me sick. Bob, spitting fire, told me I was a middle-class twat and I told him he was thick and crap in bed, only one of which I knew for sure. Sweat ran down the walls. Mark rang the bell, dimmed the lights and put Marvin Gaye's *What's Going On?* on the cassette player (which Tim had left in the kitchen with a note to tell us that it had been very special cooking for twenty people in a kitchen the size of a Fiat 124). Gavin transformed into kindness itself and crooned,

"You are loveable for who you are. Tell the person in front of you what you need." Someone who'd been before said, "I need love" and all at once and in the arms of strangers we realised that everyone, even Syrup on Shit, is loveable for who they are and not for what they do.

Bob and I had to get the train in the end. It was sad, leaving his car but everyone on the first train from Paddington seemed as loveable as we were even though they didn't know it. Derek met us in Didcot with some news.

1972–1976

IV

Malcolm was a student nurse with a new Saab. We'd always thought it was a bit strange but no one had dared ask him about it. Malcolm and Derek had been to their first encounter group together and it had come out that Malcolm had a private income but a very empty life. Derek had hatched a plan. He thought that it would be a good idea to start a commune and to live together in a permanent encounter group to accelerate the process of shedding the neurosis inevitably picked up from parents who were full of shit, do their best as they might. Bob, Malcolm, Derek and I went to the hospital social club to thrash out the possibilities but I fell asleep and had to get my dad to pick me up.

When I woke up in my room, with my Pre-Raphaelite posters and my *Tubular Bells* cassette, my mother was concerned. I'd screamed so hard expressing rage at the weekend she thought I'd got laryngitis. She made me some lemon and honey and asked if I'd like her to ring work to explain why I wasn't there. I scraped a voice from the bottom of a childhood full of the resentment I had just unearthed.

"That's bloody typical isn't it? You think you know me: how I am, where I'm going, what I'm supposed to be doing but you don't care about who I am."

"Darling."

"Don't you start with that hostile patronising shit. You don't mean 'darling' at all. You don't know how to love. If you did you'd be angry. Angry as I am. You're full of shit. Didn't your mother ever suggest you look at your own dirty arse?" This was completely against the hand-typed foolscap rules Miah had given us with a hug as we'd left the group.

After your Marathon: Rules for re-entry
1. Remember that the people in your life have not been on this journey. Do not try and share your experience with them until you have had time to assimilate the experience. Give them a *Conquestadoor* brochure.
2. Your parents loved you the only way they knew how. Forgive them.

My mother rushed to the bathroom with an empty glass. As she filled it I screamed,

"Right. Yeah. Turn away, you hostile bitch. You just can't face the truth."

The glass of water hit me full in the face.

"Rosie. Rosie. Calm down. Darling. Darling. James. James. Quick. Telephone the doctor. Rosie's hysterical. James, hurry! Quick." She ran downstairs with me following,

"What would you know, eh? See a feeling, hear what I feel and you're calling the fucking doctor. I don't need a doctor. I need love you stupid bitch."

"Rosie, dear. Stop. Shush." My father held the door open with his right hand and pointed through it with his left. "You heard your mother. That's enough, young lady. Go and get some air. Now. Don't you speak to your mother like that." That was the cue I needed.

"And you. Why don't you think for yourself and stand up to her? All my childhood I've been daddy's little girl. It's all your fault. You need to take responsibility for your own shit. And I'm going now anyway. This place is stifling. All you care about is what I do. Not who I am. I'm leaving. Now. For good. To be with people who really dare to love."

I took responsibility and gave my dad the keys to the 2CV. It was his really. I put my greatcoat over my caftan, put my jeans, the afghan and my cassette in a bag and left home. I went to the famous Swan Hotel and watched people craning their necks for a sight of Danny La Rue while I phoned Derek from reception. We had a couple of vodka and blackcurrants and went back to the nurses' home.

Derek had a new girlfriend, Lynda, who was staying with him nearly all the time in Moulsford Manor. Things were changing pretty fast but Derek said that love couldn't run out and I could stay in his room as long as I wanted and that Lynda would be there too. We couldn't sleep together any more anyway, because we'd discovered that it was inauthentic to deny the feelings of anger, jealousy and rage that we all felt in response to open relationships. Lynda and Derek had made a proper commitment. On the marathon, Bob had decided to get back together with his old girlfriend, big tits Sara. They were going back to London soon to look after his mother when she came out of prison. Making a commitment was all the rage.

Lynda had been to her first group a week before I'd been and she was full of love and real feelings. She helped me find a sleeping bag and get a few cushions together and she put Santana on repeat at night so I couldn't hear them shagging. I could but I pretended not to.

We had a barbecue by the river one night for the pantomime people. The dwarfs got very pissed and decided they'd all go to a group together the following weekend. Dopey, the clever one, managed to get Mary, a Nun who was on work experience in the hospital, to snog him. She was in such a state that Derek and I had to explain that it was okay for her to follow her heart, not her head and we took the lid off a Party King can and collected the money for her to go to the group too.

Plans for the therapeutic community for normal healthy neurotics were coming together and Derek had drawn up some rules. The first was that Malcolm had to sell his shares, relinquish his private income and buy a big house in the country. Malcolm's mother wasn't too keen. She was already upset because he'd split up with his wife, longhaired Helen. Malcolm and I went to Poole to talk to her.

His mother was surprised to see me. She said,

"Why couldn't you bring Helen? Who's this fat little thing?" I remembered Miah's re-entry rules, which was easier with someone else's mum than my own. We had cauliflower cheese in a symmetrical garden and he had to explain there was more to life than security and that he'd only married Helen to please his mother.

"What tosh," said his mother. "You married her because you wanted to have sex."

"Look, Mother. I've been on a group and I'm living my own life now," he said.

"And whose were you living before? My word, you young people. You sell your shares and I'll jump under a train."

"Fine. Go ahead and -"

"Malcolm. Go easy," I cut in, "she's doing her best."

"And you can keep your two-pennies' worth to yourself,

you little tart," said the sweet little old lady.

We realised that if we wanted to change the world we had to start with ourselves. Malcolm's mother was too frightened to take responsibility for her feelings. We knew how to follow our hearts.

I never went back to Derek and Lynda's and by the time Malcolm got the money and the house together, we'd fallen in love.

1972–1976

V

Fifteen of us moved into Potters Farm Therapeutic Community for Normal Healthy Neurotics, Blewbury, Oxon, on 15 November 1975.

Derek had been on a month-long encounter group in Germany with Vamoosh, the god of addiction therapy for the non-addicted and the man who had taught Gavin Machim all he knew during detox, training and graduation at The Last Chance Foundation. Derek, who knew what to do, drew up the rules. We structured the house so there could be "no avoiding". For the first six months there had to be two dormitories, one for women, one for men and no lock on the bathroom door, so if you went in there for sex with your partner or a shower and someone wanted to use the toilet it could all go on at once.

There were 'pull-up slips' and a box to put them in, in the kitchen, so that if anything pissed you off during work meditation, the new name for chores, you could carry on washing-up or gardening and just write down what you were feeling about someone else, knowing then that you would have to face your real feelings in the evening encounter group. Usually if you really despised someone it was because they were just like you. It was painful but at the end of pain there is joy or god or something.

There were rotas and if there was no toilet roll you could write a 'pull-up' for whoever was supposed to be on toilet awareness and they would be reminded not to space-out. Every small moment of unawareness was a gift because "the truth shall set you free" (St John, Mark Weatherby, 1975). The main thing was to be honest, which meant telling everyone what you would really feel if you were a normal healthy neurotic.

The groups were in the front room at first. The next-door neighbours, who were uptight and repressed, projected their rage onto us and imagined murders and ritual sacrifices. They sent the police round twice before we made rough but quite effective shutters from the bedroom doors and hospital mattresses. We were in encounter groups all night sometimes. Some people were so attached to their images and their games that the rest of us might have to shout for a couple of hours before they had the break through to pure pain, which was the same as pure love.

Once, Stan the Virgin had expressed his hostility and undermined the strength of the community by failing to write 'butter' on the board when it ran out even though he was on supplies meditation.

"I forgot," he said.

"You repressed piece of shit," said Lynda. "Just because you can't get laid, you ugly little git, you want to take your shit out sideways on all the women in the community through the butter."

"Arsehole," said Roger (Doc) who had little respect for virgins.

"If you really cared you'd think about it before you ate the butter, not afterwards," said Mary the Nun.

"You know, I know that I'm not taking responsibility because my mother used to try and control me by doing everything for me," said Stan the Virgin.

"Bullshit," said Derek. "You want to make excuses for yourself, you go and get an avoidance addicted power-crazed doctor to sign you in to the fucking bin." Derek's courage had cost him his career in psychiatric nursing. He had shared an insight with the chief consultant-psychiatrist that this figurehead's fear of his own repressed homosexuality had infected hospital staff who were, in turn, acting-out his hostility, which was why the place was so full of wankers. Derek lovingly reminded Stan the virgin, "You know what? You're full of shit." Malcolm wanted to try something else.

"This isn't getting anywhere," said Malcolm. "We need to get through his defences and we all care enough about him to do this for him. We can all grow from this. Sort out the circle of cushions and we'll have a 'synanon', you know, like the end of a marathon? It's getting late."

It was eerie but we knew we had to do it. Everyone looked pale and sweaty and it was really cold getting stripped off but screaming makes you hot and fear makes you cold. There was no point resisting or the whole thing would be a waste of time. We got in the fray and made our fists. Someone went first,

"You sick little piece of shit" and we were off. The trouble was there was no Mark Weatherby to switch on the Marvin Gaye and we were at it for nearly four hours before Sara, attention-seeking, said,

"I need love." And I said,

"Typical of you, you clingy, energy sucking, attention seeking fucking child," but Malcolm started crying and we all got round him in a circle to hug him and in the middle of it all Stan the Virgin started dancing and laughing and throwing himself around the room.

"I get it. I get it. I love you. I need love. Love is the answer. Wow."

Derek put on The Temptations and we celebrated that Stan had got it and that the therapeutic community was really helping us free ourselves from the sins of seven generations and so grow. We opened the shutters. It was dawn so we put the speakers through the window and carried on dancing in the garden. The milkman tapped me on the shoulder,

"Would you tell who's ever the one on milk-bill awareness this week, love, it'll be £3.37, Friday? Cash on the step's ok."

1972–1976

VI

The postman leered at Claire who'd been trying to get him to
do a group and was hanging out the washing in a fur coat and
moon boots. It was February and we'd been waiting for snow.
He dropped a letter through the door for Derek.

Beloved Derek.

Love.
Your letter reached to Bhagwan and His Love is there.
Your new name will be,
Swami Anand Premda
The bringer and sharer of love.
Now, drop the past.
Wear clothes only in the colours of the rising sun and
use only the beautiful new name that Bhagwan has given.
Do not allow identification to attach to this new birth.
Now is all there is.

Love and his Blessings.

The next page was from Bhagwan himself. Beautiful Sanskrit and a signature under Premda's new name that made the oceans seem too small. Something else was happening now that we couldn't quite put our fingers on but no one ever called Premda Derek again.

1976

Once Premda's new name had been given, clothes worn only in the colours of the rising sun and identification with the past dropped, the concept seemed to spread like wild-fire. Bhagwan sent a name for the commune too and Potters Farm became Tushita, which means heaven. Everything went orange. I found that by dropping connection with the past I could simultaneously shed the humiliating association of my name, Rosie, with the encounter group's image name, Daddy's Little Girl, and properly grow up, at last. I became, overnight, a great mover and shaker when I became Ma Prem Niyati, destiny of love. Malcolm was transformed, at a stroke, into Swami Anand Mondeo: blissful madness.

"By all means possible to free our people," I would quote, imagining the activist Malcolm X hanging out with the awesome Gavin Machim, sharing a dandelion coffee in his home in Milton Keynes. I became known for active confrontation, and found that the more often I confronted one of the others about their negative behaviour the more rapid was my own growth. I was acknowledged, even feared, for my courage and power which was testament to my ability to give and receive love, since only a truly loving person would dare to tell others what their best friend might not.

Dreadful things went on; once we decided we could help a beautiful girl to see beyond her image and glimpse her inner self if we cut her hair. She wept, defeated, as her dark curly locks fell to the floor, but none of us could really explain how that might help. On other occasions, nurses would be lured back when the pubs closed to be penned in, unwilling captives of fifteen crazy people who liked screaming abuse at people in armchairs. Consultant psychiatrists were hoodwinked into joining therapy groups, promised an observatory role only to find themselves stripped to the skin, beating imaginary colleagues to within an inch of their lives with a tennis racket or perhaps the bellows. Dreadful was acceptable in view of the 'all means possible' edict we'd picked up from Malcolm X (via Mark Weatherby) and in the certain knowledge that the truth shall set you free, and that we were right, we roared and spat abuse with ever increasing confidence that liberation was just around the corner. A hunger grew for more extreme and radical intoxicants.

Premda, the first of the community to take sannyas and so go orange, had taken off in the spring to visit Bhagwan in the ashram in Pune wanting to find out why he had been feeling so good. He returned with a bag full of necklaces, called malas, one for each of those who had already received their new names in the post. The malas each had 108 wooden beads, in rosewood, with a round wooden locket and a photograph of our master looking out. Premda also brought a picture with him. Bhagwan had sent it. It was a line drawing, on sharp sugar paper, of a fierce looking creature: Bodhidharma. He stared from the frame and made us all feel special.

Our master had sent a mystic to inspire a revolutionary therapy group, 'The Bodhidharma Intensive' which, he'd suggested, should be run by Vamoosh, the wild man from Puerto Rico with an American accent who now lived in London, leading the way. Vamoosh had trained Gavin Machim of Conquestadoor Encounter Marathon fame and so the affectation of Gavin's Puerto-Rican-American twang became transparent. Premda, when still coarse ex-marine Derek of course, had first found out about Bhagwan from Vamoosh when he'd disappeared to Zist in Germany for a month, coming back with reinvigorated enthusiasm for the sale of Malcolm/Mondeo's shares during a lull in progress, back in '75; returning from a reunion of that same group in Germany, he had come home to the commune in a long orange robe to wait for his name in the post. It all tied together somehow and Vamoosh seemed to be a key player. It was all too bizarre for the conditioned mind to fathom so the only thing to do was to trust.

Premda had encouraged the commune to follow Vamoosh's marketing instructions for the 15-day Bodhidharma Intensive. Dutifully, we'd followed instructions, and numbers for the group swelled from 15 to 44; 15 residents @ £100 each, 23 full-fee paying additional participants @ £125 and six children for £25 a throw. Fees included radical therapy, accommodation, chemical toilet use and promised home-cooked family fare. Tushita was stuffed to the gunwales not just with the groupies but also with Vamoosh's entourage of seven staff who came to run the circus.

One Friday in August the stage was set. The house gleamed. Tushita residents, still in charge, lined up to collect the cash from each visiting stranger and pass it on to Vamoosh.

Vamoosh, 5'4", lithe, a hard nut, brought Amiya, an Englishwoman who looked as if life in the drizzle had worn rivulets into her face turning her mouth down at the corners.

Two more therapists, Satori and Samosa, she a New York Jew, he the same but from London, both suffered from hay fever and multiple allergies. They seemed to crumble when they breathed air with too little carbon monoxide in it. Consequently they chain-smoked Dunhill International to remedy things. In fact, all the staff smoked long and heavy duty-free fags while the participants suffered their withdrawals. Maya and Manman came as counterparts to the aggressive therapists. Maya, whose name meant 'illusion', weighed about 35 stone, we guessed. Perhaps Bhagwan had been unable to believe the sight of her. She was a radical re-birther and Manman, a thin and wiry energy specialist, offered aura-rebalancing skills. Drop-in visiting leaders included Hubert Hunc, a single ex-addict from Freedom House Therapeutic Community (New York) for drug addicted personalities, and Rogerio, a pervy ex-American footballer who served to guard Vamoosh.

The event traumatised us all. I cried for three days until Amiya savaged me with the truth. Locked in to the lounge-cum-group-room, mattresses bulging against the windows, the rat pack followed Amiya's lead.

"Hey. You. You pathetic little English girl. Stop fucking crying, you! You hear me? Yeah, that's right. You cut that fucking shit right out, right? You know what? You're not fucking scared, or frightened, or any such fucking bullshit. You're angry. That's right. Fucking angry. Daddy's little fucking helper. I've seen you mooning up to Vamoosh. Right? You're off your fucking pedestal now, aren't you, little Hitler? And you're pissed with all these people invading your comfy little fucking sovereignty. Right? You know what? Your shitty commune, here. Right? Your commune. Your kingdom. You don't like having visitors at all. You're about as welcoming as a fuck-off sign. And you know why? Because you can't fucking stand it, can you? Not being in charge. Right? You're toppled, lady. Toppled. You got to face your own dirty-arsed-shit now, lady. Stop your fucking whingeing and whining and all the rest of your fucking bullshit shite and get your shit out! Right?" It was harsh. I had expected to be in with the in crowd, one of the upper echelon, but we'd been divided into groups and there'd be no chance of a nod and a wink from sour-faced Amiya. I beat the cushions while the others screamed abuse but, anger out, the night had ended on a cold, shivering edge with no comfort, no Marvin Gaye, no dancing and no hugs, just a cold space on the floor of a barn, roughly converted to a group room for the summer, and a thin foam layer beneath me. Inside, dormitories only recently outlawed, Amiya slept with Vamoosh in my bed, mine and Mondeo's in the love nest we had made our retreat. They lit gentle lamps that shone through the leaves of the busy-lizzies on the windowsill and they smoked joints. Premda and Luminousah had had to confront each other about dope once, and Tushita had imposed a rule: no drugs. But Vamoosh was outside the law.

For two weeks, six children became The Tangerines: Dhyanarina, an Australian had brought a thin mousy boy with matted hair; Roger and Iris brought Saffron, sharp, six and pissed off, and Scarlet, three, round and taking no shit; Premda imported Marigold, his half-Singaporean legacy from the merchant navy; Caroline brought Laura, ripped from the green-belt comfort of her father's estate agency: and Hilda brought a German child who cried for England. This mob of marauding neglect suffered outside group rooms while inside, with no sleep for days at a time and a diet only of raw fruit and veg for comfort and to save the kitchen from fatigue, the groupies screamed, and jumped, and worked and roared their way to inner peace.

The children mocked as, blindfolded and single-filed, the

adults snaked their way, shoulder grabbing shoulder, round the village on exercise meditation. They jeered as big-man-Luminousah, famous for his role as Happy in the Panto, wearing uptight-Susan-Priyadeva's undies, played the dutiful slave. They taunted with their jam and bread and rumbled Divine Erection, virgin-Stan-Anand, when they found his secret jar of Cooper's Oxford marmalade and a spoon hidden by the compost bin.

Sexathons and marathons went hand in hand. Vamoosh organised a touchy feely group and even though I really didn't think Malcolm-Mondeo would set anyone else alight, I still wasn't prepared to be in the room with him while he tried. Vamoosh said we had to 'get to everybody' but there were special rules for couples. Since 'getting to everybody' meant writhing and getting down with everybody and since couples did that with each other all the time, they had to avoid each other but watch at least one of their partner's happy encounters. The American Footballer, bodyguard-Rogerio, had been enlisted to support the liberation of participants from repression and when I tried to escape the group's experiment with touching and feeling he barred the way, carrying me back to the centre of the melee each time I edged to the door.

I had put my foot down. I'd said "No" but Rogerio had screamed in my face that I was "an uptight, frigid, fucking piece of middle England with fucking lah-di-dah ways all puffed up and ego-fucking-centred-but you know what? You're nothing but a piece of fucking poisonous crap, girl" and sat me in a bean-bag next to another, under a spotlight. There, Mondeo felt his way around the dark, silky limbs of a South American catholic with nipples as dark as loganberries and a waist sucked in by smooth, mature, supple, tender skin. Vamoosh, with a muffled microphone, schmoozed, explaining that prejudice stopped us from having a good time with people who looked like apes. In the privacy afforded only by allowing my ego room to sneer in my secret thoughts, I dared, "OK, apes. But oriental princesses? I can't take this."

Vamoosh's anecdotes ran fast and furious.

"You know what? You're all full of shit: middle-class, uptight, expensive shit. Think about it. You're lying dozing one day and you start to feel really good. Really good, man. And there's this feeling, right. This amazing, good, mmmmmmm, feeling and you're feeling these great, massaging hands caressing you. Mmmmmm. And it feels good. Right? If it feels good, do it! Go with it! Go with it! Just say, 'Yes'. So, after a while now, you're feeling good, really good and you open your eyes. Yeah. And you know what? What do you see but the source of this good feeling, right? The masseur, yeah. The masseur is a great big gorilla. A gorilla. Then your mind starts to intervene. You're thinking. All of a sudden. Thinking. You're panicking now. No. No man. A gorilla? I'm getting turned on by a gorilla? No. That's fucked up, huh? An animal, turning me on? No.

And you know what? I got it that, it doesn't matter what, or who, or why, or where, I'm turned on. Right? I'm turned on and I'm turned on and that's it. Right? I got that, it is only the mind, the control centre that wants me to stop having a good time. Crazy, man. Crazy. What is that? Huh? Hmmmmm? And you know what? You know what you gotta do now, huh? You've gotta say, 'Yes.' That's all. Easy. Ok, you're English so if you want, if it turns you on (he laughs) if that's what you want you've got the right to say 'Yes, Please!' And that's it, right? You're just gonna say 'Yes'. Right? So. You, know? Don't you go listening to your minds. Just say yes to being turned on. Say yes to pleasure.

I'm not asking that you spend the rest of your lives, right, that you get a mortgage together, any of that shit, right?

I'm just saying hey! Come on! Join in this little experiment. Drop your mind, right? Let the mind go and let go! Let go into it and if it feels good, hey! Just say 'yes', man. And you know what? It doesn't even matter if it's a gorilla turning you on. How about that? Hmm? Crazy, huh? Think about it! Just say 'Yes'!'" Vamoosh, drawing his voice-over to a close, edged to the Sony stack in the corner, by the bucket, as body-guard Rogerio tightened his grasp on my knee, pinning me to the spot and Marvin Gaye, with volume gathering storm pace asked, yet again, what the fuck was going on.

And the kids, The Tangerines, stood, one on top of the other, turn after turn, peering through the skylight over the barn door.

BUCKINGHAMSHIRE, 2003

I wonder what real women are like. Today, I followed a fat woman in the shopping centre as she lumbered up the escalator in leggings and a velour top. I saw her, naked, in the bed, up for anything, a right laugh. I felt myself an alien. Later, I stalked a young artist walking ahead of me on the way to the clay store, swinging his hips and I saw him moving rapidly and inexpertly, lying on top of his best beloved, fumbling while she made-do politely.

1976

II

Eventually the Bodhidharma Intensive came to an end. The chemical toilets went back to Wilders of Wallingford, the therapists to another gig and Tushita battened its hatches for some time. The commune became sluggish and divided while couples moved in to rooms of their own and everyone felt just a little too frightened of the shake up there might be if they forgot to wash a cup. The mammoth encounters, the unhidden agendas, too many and too violent in their expression, although not discussed, were hard to put aside. It was as if a massacre had taken place and, once put out of sight, had been forbidden entry into everyday discourse.

A malaise fell over the house until eventually someone decided that Mondeo and I should go to Pune to the ashram to collect some juice. This might help, as it had done when Premda had brought Bodhidharma's portrait from Bhagwan. Furthermore, since Tushita was now well known as an intensive therapeutic community and visitors were starting to arrive for groups and meditations, it was felt you could not be taken completely seriously as a catalyst for change unless you had been to Pune to sit at Bhagwan's feet. There a sort of refuelling, MOT and service could be done, all at once with the promise of enhanced performance and efficiency on one's return to the West.

Once extensive back-up plans had been established, Mondeo and I left the leadership of Tushita to the others in the autumn, in an act of friendship and trust, and travelled on Qantas to India.

1976

III

When the plane landed in Bombay we were asked to stay in our seats until the health inspection officer had had time to spray the cabin with anti-infection chemicals. This took a few minutes longer that it might have done if Mondeo-Malcolm had listened to his mother and had a trim before he left. The inspection officer lifted his fuzzy red hair from his shoulders and sprayed the neck of the robe that Priyadeva had knocked up for him from some hospital towelling doused in Dylon Tangerine. It made his eyes stream and, as he could hardly walk, I had to carry all the emergency supplies of Simple Shampoo we'd been advised to take as hand luggage in case our baggage went astray. Shampoo was one of our most crucial supplies for the trip since Bhagwan was highly allergic and sannyassins, his orange disciples, could not be allowed into the ashram, the community around him, with any hint of perfume. Mondeo, streaming, was panic stricken when he realised the health inspection officer's caution had resulted in his hair smelling of fly spray, but as I turned from the

41

aeroplane steps and moved towards the terminal building I lost interest in him.

A sheet of Perspex, 25' x 25', stood barricade between runway and terminus, and against this clamoured a mass of bodies, hands and faces crushed together in gestures of pleading. The air was thick, putrid and yellow, the smell hot, oily and composting. The officials hurried us past into a tin box with signs in Urdu and English and officials in shorts and long socks spitting red betel juice on the tarmac floor. The suitcases came on a cart. Three men in red loincloths heaved them into the middle of the hut-hall and we scrambled for ours. A thin man in a white loincloth pre-empted our move towards the cases and darted for them.

"Stop. Stop," said Mondeo.

"Baksheesh Baba, Baksheesh, Baba," and we got it straightaway. He would carry the bags and we would pay. He delivered them to a table in front of a man smoking what I thought was a rolled tobacco leaf and Mondeo extended an arm, offering a five rupee note. The man with the leaf grabbed it from Mondeo before our porter could take it. There was some argument and he handed it back to Mondeo.

"No, sir. No, sir. Paese, paese. Money." Five rupees was I think about 25 pence. The official was telling us a penny would do. We had no change. The porter didn't hang around and the same process went on again and again with each of the other passengers in the several hours of our waiting to move on to the next leg of our journey.

I was hot, tired and hungry and I cried for my father.

Our bags had to be scrutinised. We had a tape recorder and its value had to be stamped in our passports. If we tried to leave India without it we'd be asked to pay.

"How much?" I asked. The official waggled his head from side to side.

"How much. memsahib? Tax. Tax, Sony, very high. Bring it and we see. Now. Baba." He gestured to Mondeo and pointed to a chair for me. Mondeo had to go and fill in some forms in triplicate, which meant three desks so three queues. A boy came with some glasses full of thick, dark tea on a rough wooden board carried on his head. I gave him the five rupees and he beamed. I drank what tasted like muddy syrup and cried some more.

When they let us go we had to walk through an L shaped tunnel made from Perspex with a flat roof, every surface covered by hands, feet and bodies which surged towards us as we emerged, pleading with eyes, holding babies before me, deformities first. The taxi driver roped us into his black and yellow cab.

"Nice car. Mercedes. Station. Station. Let's go" and Mondeo haggled the price from £40 to £6 while I cried.

1976

IV

Pulsing India throbbed into the hotel room. Two flat platforms, two hard, straw-stuffed, sodden mattresses, loosely covered with worn greying muslin, and a fan groaning through the thick, acrid air. I tried to meditate. 'Don't drink the water! No Ice! No Ice!' the mind stressed, mantra like and I longed for a glass of Thames Valley tap water in a Director's Ale glass. A tap at the door. A small, dark, grubby Indian boy,

"Thumbs up! Thumbs Up! Yes. I get it. Five rupees." Mondeo was in charge. He took the sticky round tray, advertising sleek, black, hair oil. Two glasses, straight up and down. two curly bottles, tops off. Sticky- black-cola, India's defiance of the invading Schweppes army, fizzed. He threw the ice out of the window and I sipped the warm, fake coke, flies licking the rim of the cloudy glass taunting my lips. I cried. I slept.

When I woke again, the buzzing swelter flooded the room. Mondeo, in a tangerine T-shirt and Premda's similarly glorious longhi clinging to his waist, preened a carrot-tipped beard and shook water from his fuzzy head.

"Just witness your feelings, Niyati. Let go. Breathe." He scratched his freckled rashy arm, fiddling with his Seiko watch, mopping sweat creeping through eczema around his wrist. He'd a small canvas bag with a long shoulder strap holding two passports and a small tapestry purse full of strange, light coins, like those I remembered belonging to Streatley C. of E. Primary School's post office set, with two crumpled five rupee notes, each torn in three places, stuffed in the top. I knew it couldn't be as bad out there as it had seemed the day before. Another tear escaped.

Banyan trees. Juice bars. A man on a trolley with huge lips but no legs and one arm, peering up skirts. Small rolled tobacco leaves, beedies. Red-stained spit. Oranges. Bullocks. Boys running ragged, chasing the trail of valuable dung, piling it on tin trays, tall, on their heads. Rabid dogs. Children with their mother and four striped bags, perched on a small scooter, proudly manoeuvred by dad who frowned blankly into the oncoming traffic. Decorated lorries, incense-heavy. Moto-rickshaws. A mass of spikes, chains and black dusty oil metamorphosed from an army of spiders to bicycles competing for the filthy path.

Mondeo and I pushed the hotel door open and stood at the top of three steps. A woman rotated her baby's stained face towards us and pushed two fingers under its armpit, lever-like, exposing a missing hand. The woman turned her face away from the child, slumping her head onto her free, opposite shoulder, pleading while rubbing her stomach beneath the folds of her faded, sari – blue cotton, ragged, ripped, real.

"Rupees. Rupea," a smile, "Bread. No eat. No eat," the four words, tools picked for business trading from an unwritten phrasebook. Three moto-rickshaws stopped, each with an identical driver in browning white pyjamas, betel nut reddened smiles beckoning,

"Ashram. Memsahib. Bhagwan! Bhagwan!" laughing. The god who smiled. The big joke. Mondeo steered me past two children, running and pointing at their wrists, "Time? What is the time?" over the long dusty kerb into the beige-bench seat of a fourth rickshaw. It wouldn't have mattered had we wanted to go somewhere else. The long swinging rows of 108 wooden beads, aquiline profile silhouetted in circular wooden lockets, clothes only worn in the colours of the rising sun, was all the direction the driver would follow to take us to Hillside.

The path to the ahsram was littered with blankets spread on the ground with moneymaking enterprise: six guavas and newspaper-wrapping on one; beedies on another; three glasses, a chipped glass orange squeezer and a child running a muslin rag around the rim of a fourth glass, a makeshift cafeteria another. Between these stepped the Western youth moving, as if in slow motion, through another world. Nobody spoke, the meaningless attachment to the pleasantries of the phatic-pair miraculously transcended. The gates to the ashram reminded me of an elephant. They were of heavily stained rosewood, studded with brass and topped by a gold-encrusted canopy, which announced the ashram. Just inside, the first commandment, printed in black and white and pinned to a stand similar to those used to guide parents from the school car park to a speech-day marquee, reminded the unconscious jet-lagged that 'shoes and minds must be left at the gate'.

I followed Mondeo inside the ashram gates, up the steps and onto the veranda of a large, grey house.

"We are from Tushita Therapy Commune," I began but no one took any notice. Premda had had some dog tags engraved with one word, 'Tushita' and these hung round our necks from leather thongs above our malas so that we might be distinguished from other less committed seekers. Mondeo and I saw ourselves as pioneers, and Mondeo had even risked his mother's life, relinquished attachment to his private income and bought the house. I thought he commanded respect but no one seemed to understand.

A fat South African, Venus, with crazed eyes and a hot business smile, explained that we should return to the gate and buy a ticket for the Meditation Camp. We should also enrol with Central Records before making an appointment, through Leela, for darshan, a meeting with the master.

We did as we were told.

I felt sick. I didn't like it but I knew that was just resistance. I sat on a bench in the garden and Trevah drifted past and stared. He didn't say hello and I was struggling not to say, 'Trevah, I've heard so much about you. How nice to meet you. How do you do?' Trevah was famous for running the ashram's version of Gavin Machim's encounter groups and word was that, controversially, Trevah had dispensed with the rules. This meant there were no stepladders to simulate orgasm in the Pune group rooms and that if someone needed to murder their mother they wouldn't just be given a cushion to hit. Instead you might get beaten by some large German sannyassin, with her bare hands, if your mannerisms reflected the uptight and repressive neurosis of those Thames Valley parents who didn't know how to love properly. I really hoped Trevah didn't think I looked neurotic.

Ma Yoga Leela, Bhagwan's personal secretary and therefore in charge of deciding who could go to darshan and when, was tiny, dark and Indian, a rarity amongst those close to Bhagwan. Her dark eyes shone, her mouth wider than her face when she smiled and her hands moved like swallows in the spring.

"So. So there is a feeling to see Bhagwan?"

"Yes. Yes please."

"How long the stay?"

"Sorry?"

"Here is Niyati. In Pune. How long will the stay be?"

"Oh. Ha." A nervous laugh. "Three or four months."

"Very Good. Very Good. And Niyati is coming from where?"

"Tushita."

"Very good." At last. Leela moved her head from side to side and ran her hands across the large polished desk in front of her. To the left, a large diary, covered in the finest green leather. She turned the pages.

"Darshan will be happening, October 21st. Good. No scent. OK?"

"Yes. Yes. Thank you."

"And Swami? Same, same?"

"Yes, please Leela," said Mondeo.

"Very good. October 21st." Then began the ritual.

Bhagwan had elected to stay in his body, against all the odds, after enlightenment. Consequently his frame was fragile and allergic to the conditions of physical existence, top of the list of contraindications an allergy to soap and perfume. A constant battle must have raged between the drive to let go of the physical, and the drive inherent in self-actualisation to remain and offer a glimpse of non-being to others. Two expert sniffers sniffed nightly, one each side of each disciple booked to pass through the gates to Aum House, and a meeting with the master, in the dark, still evening, as crickets chirruped and frogs croaked around his open back porch. Not a trace of cosmetic could be permitted to cross the boundary.

Mondeo and I washed and scrubbed and sat rigidly, arms

held stiffly at 45-degree angles to the body in order to limit the inevitable sweat in humid, acrid, Hotel Shalimar Room 5. We had dried our hair in the sun after two washes in Simple Shampoo and seventeen rinses in water boiled in a pot on the kerosene stove Mondeo had picked up in town. The day dragged and we washed again, waiting until the last moment to unwrap two freshly washed and ironed orange robes, sealed against contamination.

In good time, we flagged down a rickshaw and arrived to sit in the ashram garden and wait. Trevah was prowling again and I broke into a sweat and then worried in case anxiety smelt like Mum deodorant. The Kundalini meditation, an hour-long physical work out that involved shaking, dancing and standing, had just finished. Fifty shaken orange seekers drifted from the large, canopied, marble floor behind the grey house and Leela's office. The path to the gates of Aum House, Bhagwan's home, wound around this open space. As we passed, dawdling meditators smiled enviously, the ego admitted on this occasion. We were going to see Bhagwan.

Special disciples stood either side of the gate: Manteesa, serious and sleekly dark-haired-dark-eyed, and Krishnu, chief protector, menacing and once Scottish. When the signal came they started sniffing. A tense time. A temperamental Irish sannyassin moved away, disgruntled and dejected when Krishnu felt a trace of fishy-soap could be detected. But if you passed the test they let you through with a stern reminder that there was to be no coughing, moving or doing anything other than was instructed.

The large house was completely hidden by jungle plants. Low lighting threw shadows across a crazed marble path, which led to a large, semi-circular back-porch, open to the garden at the sides and canopied. The floor shone: there was not a speck of dust here in this phantom space in India. A quiet and solemn orange girl led me and Mondeo to a designated spot on the floor, close to the solitary chair that faced us. Careful lighting. Clicking cicadas. Two officials held clip-board lists of conundrums which sannyassins had submitted in advance, hoping Bhagwan might furnish them with solutions. These same go-betweens held up-to-date details of therapy groups on offer and designed to set the visitors free, which Bhagwan might recommend in response to any neurotic enquiry.

Greek Manathi sat on the floor, sweeping the area around the chair with a spidery gaze, hands darting to remove stray beasties.

Hush.

Suddenly he entered. Breathtaking. He moved invisibly, grace incarnate.

One by one, sannyassins sat before him. Awe.

I felt washed by a cool breeze and when it was my turn he turned off the voice in my head. I had no words for what happened. When my children were born and even decades later, I called it love.

1976

V

The day after darshan with Bhagwan, I walked slowly to the ashram, thinking about what he'd said: 'to miss this moment is to commit suicide'. What could he mean?

Bicycles weaved between painted lorries, which lumbered towards the river. Under the railway bridge, on the dry embankments, families squatted some distance from ramshackle, makeshift conglomerations of gathered debris, their homes; roofs were made from plastic bags, covered bamboo, pasted with dung; the sides from corrugated iron; floors, blue plastic sacking, frayed; earth dissipated into dust moving beneath feet. Children followed.

"Rupea. Rupea. Baksheesh, Memsahib. Carry bag. Bag carry?" I kicked out at them with my new leather feet, cheap dyed thongs rubbing and staining between my toes. Irritation. These wise feral children disrupted my vision of India, its trees' strange roots growing from branches in regressive evolution. Thick smoke gushed from battered black and yellow taxis, crossing the railway track, carrying pressed and ironed German and American sannyassins backwards and forwards, to and from the pristine serenity of Bhagwan. Two local men walked to work hand in hand, each with a coarse hessian bag burrowing in to an outside shoulder, browning cloth kicking between their legs, white, western shirts, press-ironed, taking precedence above.

A man in uniform gazed from the gates of the Blue Diamond Hotel where palm trees stood erect above him and a gardener waved a hose at a bedraggled centre- piece, round which skirted an air conditioned coach. Harsh, lush, green grass that looked like the plastic imitation used by the greengrocers in the Thames Valley, mocked the barren road beyond the hotel gates. In the middle of the road khaki-man, in thick wool socks and shorts, directed the traffic, a menacing oiled and blackened moustache co-ordinating with his truncheon, cutting him into St George's quadrants and highlighting the central, thin, pale, whistle blowing between his teeth. To the left and to the right stalls, Punch-and-Judy-like, revealed row upon row of bark, powders, betel nut and leafy bowls tied with thin strands of black cotton, bearing crushed powders of white, green and black. Red spit on the path. Somewhere, a boy shining shoes and a chai-wallah with a steaming beaten aluminium vat full of hot, sweet, spicy tea. A table, two glasses, a boy with a rag, swilling and mopping before each new customer.

I turned into Hillside. It seemed further today, the walk towards the quiet familiar rigidity of the cool, perfect marble of the Aum House back-porch-lecture-hall. Through the gate I went, clutching my beads, my mala, terrified that I might lose this badge of non-identity.

Scores of pairs of sandals lined up in stacked boxes just at the end of the path as two regimental sniffers determined between them who should and who might not be allowed entry to Aum House and the morning discourse. Sannyassins filed in singly to take their places on the cold, hard, floor, forming semi-circular rows before Bhagwan's static chair, like the billowing ripples of a pond after the pebble sinks. Scottish Krishnu, erect, on-guard and waiting, stage-left; Greek Manarthi, sitting, sweeping the floor with her hands; Bhagwan glided, entering stage right.

It was Hindi camp. I had no idea what he said. A few select indigenous seekers chuckled intermittently; two swooned and one screamed in ecstasy and had to be dragged out roughly, while the master carefully delivered 90 minutes' spontaneous discourse. Sitting silently, doing nothing, spring comes and the grass grows by itself. The imperial language worthily took its turn and turn about with Hindi, on a 15-day cycle.

Stiff from sitting silently, without wriggling, coughing or talking, Mondeo and I left the ashram and Seville Court to find a café some way down the road towards the river, where railway-sleeper trestle-tables hung over long wooden benches. In the corner, a large kerosene stove supported a wobbling pot of simmering water. To the left, bound together, a slatted bar served as pulpit to the proud proprietor. There he stood, waving his hands so rapidly his long fingers shook together like a fan and every now and then one finger escaped to point accusingly at one of three hired, tired boys, each with a tea towel dangling from a red waist band holding up loose rough cotton-linen-mix khaki shorts. A uniform. These three chased from table to table, taking orders and scurrying back to deliver, frequently, the wrong thing.

I ordered glass Nescafe, no sugar, and papaya curd. Slimming. A tall, greasy glass arrived frothing with reconstituted Nestles baby-milk and a proud floating spoonful of powdery and un-dissolved coffee powder cushioned in the bubbles; the bowl of curd, glass-rimmed with smeary finger stains, stood in the centre of the vast orange papaya.

We talked about home. Dharma, nature-boy, had been left in charge of the kitchen department. Tushita had become the supplier of fine, homemade, stone-ground, whole-wheat loaves and rolls to the local health food shop. They had asked us to look into marmalade as they thought it would be quite quirky, coming from the orange people. It was quite a meditative challenge, though. The setting point of marmalade had caused my mother many a sleepless Sunday afternoon. Her ego seemed to rise up like the bread dough; we'd find out if our own egos were actually still in residence as we marketed our brand. We'd managed to be meditatively surrendered in the very early stages but when called upon to produce 100 jars we could be in for a nasty surprise. It was a bit like taking a driving test once you'd already been granted a licence: tempting fate perhaps. Dharma would have risen at 5am to supervise the pounding of yeast into dough. I longed for one of the hot buttery melting cottage-buns with the new bitter marmalade and some tea. Quietly, and in secret, I preferred my mother's marmalade. Mindful of the ego's underhand means of leading one astray, one struggled to detach.

Days turned to weeks and the pace of life dimmed with damp/dry ease through monsoon and Diwali, as the rhythm of ashram life crept in: meditation; discourse; walk to breakfast through the shortening shadows; meditation; lunch; meditation/conversation; sleep; meditation; discourse; walk to breakfast, paces quickening in the marketplace, the bereft and the newborn, the decorated and careworn fighting for a path. A restless ambivalence settled on my heart; I might stay, I might leave and the way forward was as yet unclear. Mondeo, in darshan, had been given some advice about networking with other sannyassins, just like us. Tushita might benefit from extending invitations to a wider world, something like that.

After discourse, after breakfast, inside my long red robe, which fell from a yoke just above my bust and bit into my sleeveless arms, I felt my stomach. I still had a roll of fat above my stretchy, Marks and Spencer's cotton knickers, the knickers I'd dyed in the tainted, rubber-sealed twin-tub in Tushita's tiny scullery with tangerine wash-in-dye. This roll of puppy-fat hung like a silent reminder that I wasn't a proper grown-up woman, and I wanted to get rid of it. As I walked away from the café, with Mondeo, sore feet dusty through the abject poverty of others' lives, I counted calories and hoped the heat would dissolve my secret.

We had to go to the back of the Rainbow Café some way away on the corner of a busy crossroads because Whayve and Sunami had a really nice room in a sort of attic, open to a corridor, which we hoped to take over when they returned to the West. I felt on home ground. Whayve and Sunami ran the sannyas centre in Leeds so they would surely recognise the importance of Tushita's transformation from 'Potter's Farm Therapeutic Community for normal healthy neurotics' to 'Tushita Therapy Commune'.

We took a rickshaw in the end, the heat and disorientation winning. The Rainbow Café was made out of corrugated iron. It had an extended fenced area, also made out of iron, and it reminded me of the pigsties I used to look into from high up on a Tappins school bus, on the Downs between Streatley and Didcot. Inside the pen the usual small boys washed and scraped. Looking in, women grovelled, showing off their mutilated babies. The menu here included such things as Baked Vegetable, so the place was mobbed with homesick youth devouring carrots in cheese sauce. Beyond, rows of bicycles stood in line beside a large hotel where square-footage had been altered to accommodate the influx of money coming to visit Bhagwan, in rooms the size of toilet cubicles.

Mondeo stopped and asked a young Dutch sannyassin, who was just unlocking a bicycle distinguished from the others only by a twist of leather on the tab under the saddle, if he knew how to find Sunami and Whayve. Of course he didn't because social chitchat wasn't necessary, or because he knew plenty of people who spoke Dutch. But he knew how to find the room. A Swiss sannyassin had attached the front of a chalet, made out of bamboo and twine, to the back of the hotel. We climbed a bamboo ladder to the eaves. Inside, a large coir mattress covered in muted orange silk squares supported Sunami and Whayve, sitting in meditation, so we joined them and made a circle.

As far as I knew, the mind was too noisy for silent meditation; that was why we had so many open encounter sessions at Tushita. Whayve and Sunami must therefore have been full of shit; she, Sunami, seemed really serene and Whayve had those piercing eyes that let you know that he could see straight through you. The roll of puppy-fat didn't help me to relax in the challenging conditions. To top it all, Sunami and Whayve had decided to stay. What a thought. They were abandoning the sannyas centre in Leeds - what would Bhagwan say? And they were not letting the room.

A postcard came from Sufi, formerly Iris, mother to Saffron and Scarlet. Sufi (Iris) and Saturn (Roger) had stayed on as residents once the Bodhidharma Intensive had come to an end. Saffron, who was now seven and Scarlet, four, of course stayed too. The postcard arrived with Suggeet, a thin wiry man who seemed to fly off the ground as he stood, balancing on the edges of alternate feet. Suggeet, a visitor and thus worth £125, was famous in Bodhidharma for sweeping against the wind and covering himself in dust, leaves and chicken shit. Vamoosh had put him in charge of maintenance tasks and he'd stood, shoulders hunched to his ears, a stretchy orange T-shirt flapping at the top of each scrawny arm, and witchery fingers, deeply stained under the nails, clutching a clipboard as a knight holds a shield, his pen his sword. A little bit of power.

"Hi, Niyati."

"Suggeet. Hi. You've just come from the West?"

"Yeah. It's so good. I went to Tushita. Everyone's looking *really good.* Yeah."

"Good." I bristled.

"I've got a card here for you." His sentences intoned upwards at the end. Creep.

"It's from Sufi. Yeah."

"Thanks. Yeah. You doing groups here, Suggeet?"

"Yeah. Yeah. Rebirthing, Tantra and Encounter?"

"Fuck." He must be really fucked up if Bhagwan's making him do those.

"Yeah."

"Ok. Yeah. Thanks Suggeet. Good."

The postcard:

Hiya Niyati.
Just to let you know. Saffron was having nightmares so Saturn and I have moved in to yours and Mondeo's room. Priyadeva has taken over household maintenance and we've created some new work meditations. So everything is changing and it's really good.
Love. Sufi.

It was typical of Suggeet to bring such a postcard, sideways hostile weak shit, a red rag to a bull.

"Mondeo. I don't like it."

"Trust, Niyati. Trust."

"You know what? You really piss me off with your fucking trust. Fuck it. She's being fucking hostile and you know it. That possessive mother shit's a fucking weapon. Invading my space. Fucking bitch." I didn't really know very much about children. When they'd been overly intrusive, going on about drinks and food and stuff, during Bodhidharma, I had realised their parents were really fucked up.

We had been in Pune for three months when, on reflection, considering the upended approach Whayve and Sunami seemed to have adopted and their almost lethargic attitude to growth and feeling that there was work to be done in England which could really be ignored, realising that the dynamism we had at Tushita was unique, and since we'd accomplished what we'd come to do, we decided that we really ought to go back. I felt terribly important but I had, by then, forgotten why.

1977

Luckily, when Mondeo and Niyati arrived home from India, Sufi and Saturn, the fucked-up parents, were in the middle of a nasty confrontation. He said she was clingy and possessive, she that he was a fucking slag. There were cups all over the house and Priyadeva had to be confronted straightaway since the blackboard list of roles announced that she was still in charge of the kitchen. Everybody said that Niyati was beautiful and soft but still strong and that Mondeo had shifted some of his (uptight) repressed uptightness to be a little bit crazier, which was a good thing.

Although things had moved on quite considerably in three months, with local interest growing in stone ground bread and our new range of bitter marmalade, (apparently there had been no confrontations at all during product development and Niyati and Mondeo's absence) and Londoners paying well for short breaks for active mediation and to revisit sites of original, primal pain, everyone was keen to know what Bhagwan had said. As far as they could understand, they were aware that he wanted them to get some new blood in through the door. They had a couple of spaces for residents, Premda and Punani having left to settle permanently with Vamoosh, and it seemed a good idea to spread the net more widely and find others who were like them. After all, Bhagwan had said that they should 'issue an invitation to the unknown'.

A poster was placed in the sister centre, Khatahpult, a meditation centre in London.

Tushita Therapy Commune for normal healthy neurotics. Bhagwan's name for our commune, Tushita, means heaven and extremes cannot live divided. If you will live in hell with us and surrender to a committed process of self-discovery and shedding the ego, apply to: Ma Prem Niyati, Tushita Therapy Commune for Normal Healthy Neurotics, Blewbury, Oxfordshire.
Please send a photocopy of your letter from Bhagwan showing your sannyas name.

No sooner had the invitation to the unknown been placed than the letters poured in. There were three but two were eliminated for expressing antagonism: one in the form of suggestions that Tushita entertain soft therapies such as yoga and the other in a veiled attempt to usurp Tushita's uniqueness by referring to the Findhorn Garden. The third held greater promise than the commune had hoped the unknown might offer up.

The house was buzzing. Anand (Stan the virgin), demoted yet again to toilets, had gone into such a state of surrender while polishing the taps that Niyati was moved to ring the gong for a spontaneous group hug, in celebration of the shine he had produced. She had been simmering kidney beans and shelling a new crop of broad beans, in preparation for lunch with Avalon and Sacharina, a couple and the only applicants invited to attend an interview, when she'd popped in to the downstairs loo to wash her hands.

Avalon, a legend from the encounter movement who had trained with Vamoosh and Gavin Machim in the Last Chance Foundation for drug addicted neurotics, and Sacharina, an unknown South African sannyassin, had just returned from Pune where they'd met. There were no particular criteria to be met by those wishing to join Tushita other than total surrender. This meant submitting to the unwritten code, drawn almost exclusively from Gavin Machim's encounter marathon rules: no violence, no drugs, no leaving and no disagreeing with whomsoever had undeclared supremacy (usually Mondeo and Niyati who agreed with each other) over everyone else.

Ideas about sexuality had to recognise and reflect respect for the incredible door to the divine that might be opened during an orgasm, especially in view of Reich's dire warning that people who don't have orgasms are really dangerous. (Also, since Premda had been to India again and had it off with a German sannyassin even though he was in a relationship with an Englishwoman, nobody believed it was a good idea to be monogamous anymore. It was just lucky that Mondeo's latent catholicism would allow him only to fancy Niyati and that she didn't really 'get' all that about free sex yet.) Even though Avalon had expressed concern over the developing habit of what he termed, rather defensively, 'promiscuity' it was still felt his skills as a trained encounter group leader would be an invaluable asset in encounters and impromptu marathons. The community felt that Bhagwan had sent them yet another gift, in the nick of time.

Preparing for the encounter with Avalon and Sacharina, Niyati was confident in her role, having firmly established her matriarchy by reminding Sufi, who had attempted to usurp her position as soon as she'd moved in (with her bloody kids,

61

after the Bodhidharma Therapeutic Community experience), that she had elected to delay her own personal growth through giving birth to Saffron and Scarlet. This choice rendered Sufi impotent, leaving Niyati without challenge to her role as super-surrendered-virtually-ego-free-assistant-director of Tushita, especially since she and Mondeo were totally committed to each other, albeit in a non-possessive way, and his name was on the deeds of the farmhouse. Taking off her apron and pulling two wings of hair over her too-rosy cheeks, she turned to find Avalon watching her from the kitchen doorway.

"Very nice, Ma. Very nice." Middle English with a Puerto Rican twang.

"Hi. Wow. You must be …"

"Avalon"

"Wow. I'm Niyati. Well, I am not Niyati but Niyati is the beautiful name Bhagwan Shree …"

"Yeah, yeah, yeah. A Rose by any other name."

"How did you know?"

"Sorry?"

"About Rosie?"

"It's Shakespeare. Hey! They told me you were supposed to be the one with a brain."

"Oh God. How embarrassing. I am trying so hard to drop the mind."

"Hey baby. There's nothing wrong with your brain, not at all. The mind, now there's another story. But the brain? That'll be the biggest sexual organ you've got, girl." Puerto Rican with very little twang at all. It was just like being with Vamoosh except that Niyati really wasn't that used to banter anymore. She didn't know how to handle this one. Apart from his clothes, a finely tailored raw silk two piece suit in vermilion with brownish flecks, he didn't look special; in fact she thought she could have seen him before but this was Avalon, after all. No wonder he looked familiar. They already knew all there was. She'd expected someone a bit older; he might have been 25. She knew that shouldn't matter, but Gavin was 31. But how could she tell if he was coming out sideways? Or was it ok just to joke about like this? Thankfully, Mondeo filled the doorway as Avalon let go of her, mmm-ing at the hug they'd just shared. Mondeo was dressed head to foot in amber towelling, a huge long robe with stretchy pyjama bottoms underneath. As he'd just blow-dried his long, red, fluffy hair, it stood around his head in a ring against the sun pouring through the door. He was nodding and smiling. Obsequiously. Avalon had reactivated Niyati's burdensome English Literature knowledge and she kept thinking about the git in *David Copperfield* that was always wringing his hands. Uriah Heep. The non-possessive nature of her love grew in stature. Mondeo took Avalon off round the grounds to show him the asparagus bed.

The commune convened round the kitchen table as Niyati ladled a beanie mush into earthenware and Dharma unearthed some day-old bread, returned by the whole food shop. Avalon looked a bit deranged, with wide eyes darting between heavy locks of dark hair which he continually pushed to the side, a Rolex, a present from Vamoosh, rattling on his wasting wrists. He carried an Italian leather shoulder bag, stuffed to the gunwales with Dunhill International; four times an hour he swivelled to reach another cigarette from this bag as it swung on the arm of his chair. No one said anything about the no-smoking in the kitchen rule, awe-struck as they were to have someone of such calibre in their sights.

Avalon was, quite surprisingly, really very negative about Pune. This last visit had been his third to India since Vamoosh had sent him straight there when he finished his training at The Last Chance Foundation, to run groups. He had alternated between Pune and Vamoosh's place in London where he'd worked with individuals if he got the chance. On this last trip to the ashram he had been unsettled by changes to the administration since his first meeting with the master. He complained of 'power-crazed bitches' and 'blood-sucking leeches' who stood between him and Bhagwan. He dropped a few comments about the money he could have been earning in London running 48 hour encounter marathons, rather than in Pune where he had, he said, been made to work seven days a week for nothing. Niyati was taken aback since she had fully embraced the concept that acceptance, surrender and saying 'yes' when every cell of your being might otherwise choose 'no' led to liberation from neurosis, identification with the past and possessive jealousy. Seeing a chance to consolidate her safe, superior standing and to advance her reputation for brave, selfless and courageous confrontation, she stood up:

"Avalon. We, here at Tushita, are committed to surrender. We recognise that we cannot know what Bhagwan's purpose is in pressing our buttons with devices such as the matriarchy that governs the ashram, and work meditations. You need to look at your own dirty arse and try to surrender." Feeling, somehow, that this lacked conviction, she added, "You're far too resistant for us," for good measure. Sacharina was down her throat like a tornado.

"For fuck's sake you stupid little English twat. Have you got any idea what it's like working for those fucking head-fuck women who run the fucking ashram?"

"Sacharina. You've got a lot of work to do with regard to women. Do you know I'm Niyati?"

"Yeah. And?"

"And" but before Niyati could stop the South African control freak, Anand-Stan-the-Virgin was on his feet,

"And she thinks she's fucking God."

Niyati slammed her knife and fork into her mouldering kidney bean stew and it splashed Sacharina's raw-silk, co-ordinated, saffron salwar kameez. Sacharina reached across the table and slapped Niyati right across the face.

"We have a no violence rule here, so we can express ourselves in safety and honesty." Niyati expressed her-no-self in a steady, centred voice, breathing deeply into her solar plexus.

"Who the fuck says so?" said Sacharina.

1977

II

It seemed unfeasible not to accept Avalon and Sacharina's offer to join the community since they had clearly been sent to press everybody's buttons, make the comfortable uncomfortable and create a shake-up, which could only be a good thing. There was general consensus that there had been a misunderstanding at that first meeting. Luminosah, tall and on the ball, pointed out that marathon leaders, like Gavin, Vamoosh and Avalon, were specially trained to support us to look up our own backsides rather than establish a precedent for us to look up theirs. Embarrassingly late we realised that it was not our job to know anything about Avalon at all. He had trained in addiction with Vamoosh just four years ago, (in the Last Chance Foundation for ex-addicts and non-addicted ex drug users, addicted to abnormally normal healthy neurosis). He had also been working with people and running groups, for normal healthy neurotics and sannyassins, for three years already.

With some trepidation but a general sense that it was the

right thing to do, Mondeo drove the orange 2CV to collect Avalon and Sacharina from Vamoosh's London flat and to somewhere near Silverstone to pick up a Bang and Olufsen stereo, from Avalon's brother's place, coming back to Tushita via the off-licence of a Wallingford pub, and the two new residents donated four litres of Merrydown to the evening meal, smoothing the way.

And a new and terrifying era in Tushita insinuated itself amongst them.

It wasn't long before it became apparent there was something terribly wrong with Avalon. On the fifth day of his residency, while Sacharina was out being interviewed as a potential nursing assistant at Fairmile Psychiatric Hospital (ECT department), Avalon asked Niyati if she'd drive him to Wallingford in the 2CV. Of course 'yes' was the only answer since 'no' was out of the question and Niyati found herself barricaded in by a round cast-iron table in the George Hotel's courtyard, with a pint of Guinness and cider to drink and Avalon before her.

Avalon explained that although Sacharina was possessive and terrified of exploring her feelings of competitive envy, he felt intuitively that he and Niyati had past-life experiences to unravel. This was a new one on Niyati and she found she couldn't quite get on board with the theory before she had drunk another half pint of the foul black mixture Avalon insisted she consume. This, he explained, would enable her to loosen the grip of her resistance and to drop identification with her most recent past and particularly her terror of upsetting Mondeo. It was clear that, although Avalon had an odd way of going about self-exploration, he had a point and as Niyati focussed exclusively on his gaze and the courage Avalon showed in the face of Sacharina's inevitable resistant defensive reactions, she found she couldn't find any feasible explanation, other than that forwarded by Avalon, for the magnetic pull he had over her. Abandoning attachment to the safety and security of exposing all actions, deeds and thoughts to the whole Tushitan community, Niyati agreed to have sex, in secret, with Avalon in room 203.

It was dank and dark in room 203 and the stickiness of the sheets reminded Niyati of an apartment in Pune where she and Mondeo had stayed for three weeks. That particular flat had, in a sense, saved her from getting on with exploring the pre-orgasmic and so dangerous neurosis buried within her, since the infestation of rats had put Mondeo off sex for the length of their stay there. Here, though, without the vermin, Avalon took his time, unpeeling the top layer of the chunky knitted orange maxi-cardi which covered Niyati's wrap-around, hot-red-silk beneath. His hands, quick and mature, fondled the fastenings on her M&S 34A, concurrently letting his own raw-silk pyjamas, in dark sienna, drop to the floor so that a stubby, mottled and urgent penis pressed into her belly button. Naked, he grabbed her shoulders and threw her, frenzied, onto the sticky polyester-mix where, in a matter of seconds, he ejaculated, missing her hopeful yet gratefully disappointed sweet young crotch.

Pre-orgasmic women and prematurely ejaculating men usually had to spend months, sometimes years, exploring their sexuality in encounter and tantra groups both in London and in Pune, to save humanity from the damage such neurosis might inflict on communities at large. Niyati, bright, horrified and in a quandary, had unearthed Avalon's secret, quite inadvertently, and the burden of her knowledge, and her guilt, bound her to hi with a sense of responsibility for him, and the world at large, which she must now shoulder completely alone.

Niyati drove Avalon back to Tushita slowly and resumed

her post as Kitchen Dominatrix in a subdued mood.

Mondeo had been to Leamington Spa for an acupuncture treatment and was lying in the bedroom with a copy of The Guardian falling across his orange-meditation-blindfold, keeping out the light. Sacharina, having successfully secured employment as a nursing auxiliary, was ironing the uniforms she would be wearing from 7am the next day when her shift began.

"Oh," said Niyati, "Grey."

"You got a problem with a fucking grey nurse's uniform?"

"I don't know. I don't know."

"And that's a first. Bugger me. Niyati doesn't know the answer for once." Niyati, thinking better of challenging Sacharina about her hostility, retreated to dig up some artichokes for dinner as Avalon eerily prowled the boundaries of the property, looking under hedges.

A bucket under an outside tap provided a confessional for Niyati as she scrubbed the knotty roots beneath the fast-flowing, shivering, silvery water and she resolved to go into silence. Putting the artichokes on to boil, she made a sign from the back of an Alpen box and used a bit of string to hang it round her neck. With one of Saffron's special green felt-tips, she wrote, 'Silent meditation. Watching the witness. Please do not talk to me.' and she thought it would do the trick.

Mashing the grey ground artichokes with raw milk and pepper, Niyati flinched as Mondeo rubbed her lower back gently with a rolled up newspaper and mouthed, silently, "Wow. Silence? You? You've gone into silence?" She nodded and scooped spheres of the watery goop onto plates before adding a baked mushroom stuffed with corn and soya sauce to each, lovingly settling the plates before the hungry seekers. Older residents, used to the economy, nodded at Niyati and tried to smile while Sacharina, and Avalon, pushed their plates away.

"You can stay as fucking silent as you like you devious little cunt," said Sacharina, "but I'm going to make a fucking scene about this shite. You expect me to eat this crap?" Niyati was shocked into deeper silence and simply gazed at Avalon, hoping that he, her secret, might jump to her defence.

"Give me the fucking car keys," he said.

"That's my car," said Mondeo.

"Well fucking drive me then!"

"Where?"

"Chinese Take-Away. And now. Come on, man. You gotta agree with me here, Man. This, I mean, Christ. Fuck me. This is worse than the fucking crap they feed you in fucking Pune." Anand started to applaud, blinking with each sharp claxon while staring straight at Niyati. Voiceless, she couldn't take it and catapulted a hot ball of artichoke directly across the table to land, splat, right in the centre of his third eye. Sacharina was on her feet, lifting the side of the table as she stood to tip its contents up at a 90 degree angle so that plates, glasses, water, Tamari, Tahini and the goopy gloop formed an avalanche to slide into the creeks and the flats of quarry tiling while Sacharina's strong right arm, yet again, directed the full force of a right handed slap across Niyati's face. This time though Niyati, fore-warned, caught the woman's arm as it rebounded in flight, swivelling Sacharina to the floor where she retained a tight grip of Niyati's jaw, sliding fingers beneath her tongue for purchase against the steep bank of her lower teeth. Niyati bit hard as blood fell in slow drips into a congealed artichoke mess on her socks. Sacharina snatched her hand away, to push herself up. She slumped in a chair.

Niyati, resolutely silent, still spoke not a word and Avalon, shaking, crawled under a large wooden chair to suck his thumb and whimper.

"Niyati. Don't leave me. Niyati."

Nobody knew what to do next. Clearly, there was a lot more shit to get out but the violence and destruction of property was not something any of them had experience of. Niyati, in silence, simply shrugged and moved towards Avalon, hoping that an experienced marathon group leader might be able to save the day. But rather, seeing her approach, Avalon hurled the chair which sheltered him across the kitchen, pulled Niyati swiftly outside through the back door and threw himself and her beneath the neighbouring hedge. From there, crouching, ready to sprint, he urged,

"Run! Run!" and, seeing no viable alternative, Niyati skittered after him to shelter in an idyllic summerhouse, overlooking a small quadrant with a pond, in Colonel and Mrs Bannister's garden next door. Niyati peered into Avalon's eyes but he seemed no longer present. Instead, a terrified child whimpered, "They're going to get me. I outwitted them. Today. They wanted, they'd arranged, I was to go with the bins. I heard them. They were putting me out. But you, you knew too. Didn't you? You saved me, so you did. You drove me to safety and wrapped me in your arms. But now; watch out!" and Avalon fled from the gazebo, crawling on all fours, head down, to cower under the hedge again.

"Avalon?" Niyati pulled at a daisy beside the path, gravel lines separating grass from the hedge. "Avalon. You know, it's ok. Like the Encounter Marathon in Pune? There's like confrontation? Well, you know, Avalon. Here, in the commune we have impromptu encounter? It's ok. There's a lot of noise. It's not very nice really but we're growing. Yeah? Well, you know, Avalon. We're growing." He wasn't even listening but pulled at the cuffs of her cheesecloth tie-dyed two-tone orange shift thrown over her red silk wrap, whimpering, his other hand wedged, thumb first, into his mouth. Niyati was out of her depth. The lights of the 2CV swung in an arc across the drive to Tushita, next door, as Mondeo drove out of the gates. Niyati just glimpsed Anand (Stan the Virgin), next to Mondeo and Sacharina's raven head in the back seat. She hatched a plan.

"Avalon. You know. Love is the answer. Yes? And I love you, right? So you and I, we'll stay close, yeah? And we're going to creep back in to Tushita, now. Yes we are. Yes. And you're going to cuddle up cosy in my bed, yeah? And we'll see what to do next later on."

"Don't leave me."

"Just follow. OK?" Bravely they navigated the hedge, skirted the back door, stooping beneath the kitchen window, running to the front door which creaked open breaking long untroubled cobwebs as it swung. Avalon, head down, muttering, crawled up the stairs behind Niyati. She, true to her word, tucked him in with a cosy shawl, the radio and a packet of Dunhill International. She watched, thinking him asleep, balking at his breathing, fast paced, panicked, and wondered what to do.

Although Niyati was aware that ideas about psychiatric disorders were all articulated in relation to some fictional notion of 'normality' (and so bollocks) she was getting the distinct impression that Avalon was not fully himself. Every time she tried to leave the room to find help, Avalon clung to her with such desperation she dared not go. An hour passed with her resuming her silence to save embarrassment and Avalon using her arm as a teddy. At last, Mondeo popped his head round the door.

"Niyati. I was so worried ... Oh. Hello Avalon."

"Get that crazy fucking lunatic out of here; Judas Iscariot, Judas Iscariot," bellowed Avalon, tears streaming down two cheeks. Mondeo, recently fully qualified in psychiatric nursing, had seen something like this before.

"Niyati will stay there with you Avalon. I know that your sense is I am not OK but I promise I mean you no harm. Now. Avalon. When did you last go to sleep?"

"Judas. Fucking Judas. Fucking …" and Avalon leapt across the room, hurling himself at Mondeo, grasping, fruitlessly for his throat. Mondeo ducked, clutched both arms round Avalon's two knees and landed him safely back on the bed.

"Stay here Niyati! I will find something that I think may help." Mondeo slammed the door behind him and thundered down the stairs. A door swung open and closed somewhere, a clatter of cutlery and Mondeo's footfalls retraced a reverse path up the stairs towards them. "Right. Niyati. Give this to him, right? Benylin. Half a bottle and I'll call a meeting in twenty minutes."

Avalon, who was now entirely tied into the foetal position and tangled within the Laura Ashley duvet, whimpered as Niyati spoon fed him half a bottle of the drowsy medicine, gently cupping his head in her hands. As the evening wrapped itself around the farmhouse and the last, straggling birds pecked a twitter from the evening, Avalon slept and Niyati returned to her lair.

The table, resurrected, was strewn with greasy paper bags and foil boxes, overflowing with bean sprouts, tofu and bright yellow chicken. Everyone was there, except Anand and Sacharina but the atmosphere was more like the type you always got at meetings about how to spend money on the village hall than that of a meeting of likeminded seekers of enlightenment. Priyadeva spoke first,

"Are you going to tell her, Mondeo, or shall I?"

"Go ahead."

"You're probably wondering where Sacharina and Anand have gone, eh Niyati?" Niyati nodded. "You're not going to believe this. You're not. No really, you're not. Mondeo went into the Chinese takeaway to get this lot and he suggested that Anand and Sacharina just go and have a drink, in The George, right?" She nodded again, growing anxious. "But when he got there, Mondeo, with the Chinese, you know? They were like, nowhere. So he said, to the reception person, you know, um. 'Have you seen two people dressed only in the colours of the rising sun? You know, orange' and she said, get this! She said, 'Yeah. Orange! What's all this about orange? Yeah. They're up there in room 203.' Then she said, 'again.'" And Mondeo and Priyadeva kind of grinned at each other. It was actually really good news in a way, for Stan-Anand the virgin. Mondeo took up the baton.

"Yes. It seems that Sacharina, and now Anand are not prepared to live in honesty and truth because earlier, according to the receptionist although she says she wasn't the one on duty this afternoon, I digress, earlier, when we all thought Sacharina was at that interview, right? There were two people dressed only in the colours of the rising sun in room 203, briefly, this afternoon." Niyati glanced into the scullery where the ironing board stood and two grey dresses had gone up in smoke. Mondeo went on, "and we think, you know, we think that Sacharina and Anand had planned this, and we have considered they may even have hatched this plan some time ago, because, if you think about it, if you think about the way in which the encounter happened earlier? Well, clearly they had a plan because when I checked again with reception, the booking, this afternoon, was made in Sacharina's family name, yeah? Melvyn. So, it doesn't take a genius really, does it?" Niyati said nothing but she could see Avalon, earlier, handing an account card, apparently not in his name, unless, perhaps they had married for a passport, to the receptionist in The George and it seemed god was on her side and Sacharina had just done the same. Mondeo went on, "So. Right. Problem one: Anand and Sacharina will not be continuing this experiment in personal growth and human potential with us here at Tushita, since they cannot be trusted and there will be no further violence, repeat, none, ever again at Tushita. That, I think we all agree, goes without saying, yes?" Everyone, in unison, agreed, 'yeah' and Niyati, in silence, nodded, smiled and blushed. "But," said Mondeo, "I think we have a more serious issue to deal with regarding Avalon." Mondeo would always revert to Poole-Dorset formality if you rattled his cage, "and although I recognise he is perhaps suffering what we might term, in psychiatry, a psychotic episode, I feel we must not resort to labels and diagnoses in our therapeutic community so I'm going to phone Vamoosh. Agreed?"

It took a couple of hours to get Vamoosh on the phone since Amiya had answered and given Mondeo some painful hidden agendas to digest before she would listen to his enquiry.

"Oh right, you think, just because you've done a couple of groups with Vamoosh, yeah? You think you can just ring his phone? That's just what I'd expect from some stinking rich fucking carroty-English-landowner pretending to run a hippy fucking commune, giving it all fancy fucking names. You wanna think about that, Mondeo. Look inside."

"Amiya. I hear what you're saying, thank you. You know, we could really do with some advice here."

"Huh!"

"It's Avalon."

"Right. Ok. Look, Vamoosh, right. You're in luck here, ok, because Vamoosh, he might just wanna hear what you're saying if it's about Avalon, you know? He kindof takes a special interest in his ex-trainees, like, a, um, father." She coughed, "I'll see."

"Amiya, do you think, I'd be really grateful, do you think you could ask Vamoosh what he thinks about psychosis?"

"Get off that psychiatry fucking trip man. I'll see if Vamoosh feels to ring you when he has had some dinner and a bath."

"Thank you so much Amiya." He gave her the number and said "Namaste". Vamoosh, fed and watered, rang at midnight and gave Mondeo the name and telephone number of a Humanistic Psychodrama Therapist who could help.

1977

III

Days ran into weeks as they waited for the prearranged date when Simon, the Humanistic Psychodrama Therapist, would convene the group to work together to rectify Avalon's disease. In the interim, Mondeo kept guard on a small put-you-up on the landing outside his bedroom while, inside, Niyati nursed Avalon who lived, mainly, on Benylin. During the day Avalon would venture out to perch with Niyati on the rafters in the top of the group room barn and Priyadeva brought them sandwiches. Avalon's second greatest fear, the third being the bin-men, the first, Mondeo, was of birds and his main aim was to be higher or lower than they might be, should they venture inside. He would traverse open areas outside, snake-like, head down, pulling himself along on his stomach with his elbows. His fear of Mondeo was mortal; a glimpse of him would send him into a full-blown panic attack, gasping for breath and clinging feverishly to Niyati as if she were a living organ donor. At night, Avalon slept fitfully with Niyati who was almost suffocated by his koala grip. She felt like Kanga, in *Winnie the Pooh*, wishing Roo would climb out of her pouch and leave her to her own thoughts. Commune organisation had to be devolved entirely to Mondeo but Niyati's surrender to her task stood her in good stead with her peers. She also fell, hook, line and sinker, for Avalon, absent as he might have been.

Simon, the Humanistic Psychodrama Therapist, had a very nice car and no entourage, which was odd. He drank herbal tea and he didn't smoke which was stranger still. Niyati and Avalon were in the bedroom when he arrived, as arranged, and there they stayed until the commune had assembled in the group room. There, without her or Avalon, the others organised themselves in dramatic friezes indicating the power structures, relationships and fissures within the house. A space was left for Niyati in the final montage, on the inner ring of a two circled mandala. Avalon's vacant place was in the centre since, Simon said, Avalon had focussed all the energy of the community on himself.

Once the stage was set, Simon, Sujan and Luminousah, all six-footers, crept up the stairs and threw an army blanket over Avalon's head. As he lost grip of Niyati, he screamed, "Niyati, Niyati. Why have you forsaken me?" and wailed like an elephant might over a lost child. This quivering, felt-wrapped mourning was unceremoniously dumped in the middle of the group room's montage. A chill was passed in anxious glances from one to the other of the complicit, contemplating their hostage.

Simon had attached strong rope to the blanket and, walking away, whipped the cover from Avalon's head with a sharp yank. Terrified, there he was, facing those he dreaded. Avalon scrambled to the make-shift shutters, holding the foam against the windows, but the group surged to force him back to the centre where Simon, again with the rope, instructed two men to bind Avalon's feet so that they might suspend him, upside down from an ancient rafter once used for hams, to simulate rebirth into the community with a sharp slap on his behind. But Simon's ropes, bound clockwise, unwound as he spun the other way. Avalon's feet untwining, he slid to the floor and with one final dive at a shutter, no one knows how, broke through to run away, faster than anyone could say Humanistic Psychodrama Therapist. No one ever knew where he went. Niyati grieved a still-birth.

Simon was better at his job than it seemed, in a sense, since, having failed with Avalon, he ensured that all who remained felt confident of their role in the re-formed community. No empty spaces remained where Avalon had once been in the dramatic final frieze the group posed to represent their re-entry.

Re-entry, in this instance, represented progression through letting go of the past without guilt, regret or remorse. Nobody said anything about compassion. It was evident, as the montage made clear, that nothing had been lost when Avalon went.

1978

An urgency, a sense of rapid change and an insistence in the music and the press that an Aquarian age had dawned, mitigated the lingering unsaid sense of failure for them all, reinvigorating their hope of a restructured world. A new rhythm and order had to be established with interest in Tushita's bakery products and a new range of bitter-marmalade growing nationally, and Londoners as well as other Europeans paying through the nose for short breaks for active mediation and to revisit sites of original, primal pain.

Tushita, though still essentially a small group of passionate seekers, became an international centre, open and of service to all callers. This placed additional responsibility on Tushita's residents to hasten their own personal growth and progress towards enlightenment at a faster pace than the average, run of the mill, sannyassin. Although the mood of the house was far less apathetic than it had been before the invitation to the unknown had been made, and although the programme of experiential interaction continued to expand like a hot air balloon, Niyati and Mondeo felt compelled to return to Pune for yet another shot in the arm.

Pune was fuller than they had anticipated when they arrived and accommodation was tricky to find. Niyati and Mondeo moved, finally, from The Shalimar Hotel, full of Italians who argued all night long, to the veranda over the porch of a fine and splendid colonial residence in the road behind Hillside and the ashram's peace. The family below prized white skin and stayed out of the sun, teaching their children to speak the business English of the day.

A man came, on foot and daily, swinging two pots from a yoke across his shoulders: in these pans heavy pumpkins, rusty potatoes, onions, tomatoes and coriander. Niyati traded and carried warm, earthy offerings up the stone steps of the veranda. There, on the white tiled terraced floor, she fired up the kerosene stove to make pumpkin ratatouille, an imitation of her mother's ministrations, heroically conducted on a one-burner Calor Gas camping-stove in the summer of 1964. Her father had been made redundant when she was seven, nearly eight, and she'd spent five weeks roving on the hot white sands of Medina Di Carrera. Another boiling made mashed potatoes, sweet with buffalo cream and sour with rancid ghee. She was happy playing house.

The mornings and the evenings bounded the day.

Every other morning, Bhagwan answered questions that sannyassins sent in. Complex questions, such as, 'How did Tantra grow out of Buddhism which, as far as I know, views sex as a hindrance to meditation?' and 'What happens to my voice when you speak to me?' Niyati wondered about sending in a question of her own and spent most of each morning's 90 minutes trying to think of a good one. Darshan fortnightly, by appointment and in the evening, was less of a threat. A personal consultation with the master. At some point, she thought, she might ask him about sex. The truth was, Niyati didn't really like sex with Mondeo and it hadn't gone too well with anyone, ever, except with Patrick O'Connor, the sculptor-cum-gardener when she was still at school, but it was expected and what a woman did. Well, that was convention, which should be ignored, but Premda had warned her that Reich had realised that the most dangerous, fucked up and repressed people in the world were those who didn't enjoy orgasms. God forbid. She'd explored orgasmic functioning in a group in London, with a Canadian guy called Sam Walkner. Sam had encouraged her to lie on the floor and to breathe bioenergetically. This meant filling the belly on the inward breath and performing a fast, sharp, hot, forward pelvic thrust while moaning on the exhalation. Everyone in the group had gathered round and she'd been encouraged to go all the way. When she had felt as if she was about to pee, she'd given one triumphant thrust and exhaled in a frenzy only to slump to the applause and warm hugs of 15 sweaty, smelly participants. She still didn't fancy Mondeo. Perhaps it was because he was catholic; he hadn't fully explored the link between his anal fissures, his eczema and his time at the hands of the Christian Brothers. It was possible he might be really dangerous.

In Niyati's first darshan of the visit Bhagwan had advised her to join 'Intensive Enlightenment' and to do the gentle humming meditation, the 'Nadabrahma', rather than the more aggressive therapies on offer. She was to stop pushing the river; she was to start to allow the divine to enter her, becoming a hollow bamboo. Intensive Enlightenment was a three day event, held somewhere near the river. You had to sit for an hour and a half at a time, facing another. For 45 minutes one would command the other, 'Tell me who you are!' while the other sought both to keep eye contact and to come up with a range of responses. When the bell rang you had to swap roles and so an hour and a half passed. Then, for a further 45 minutes, there was work meditation or a bowl of salt-free rice and boiled vegetables. This cycle continued for 18 hours a day and at the end of three days, the layers of the onion had been stripped away to reveal the central meaning of existence. Nothing. Not something and not nothing and not either of those either. She had read Jean Paul Sartre in the sixth form and Elizabeth Flowers had painted the aimless dead, always present, pawns in the game. *Les Jeux Sont Faits*. Through Intensive Enlightenment Niyati found the endless story telling that filled the time between now and then provided a fiction through which to live her life. This, of course, accelerated the process and took her to a state of meditative being-ness that might otherwise have evaded her until she was 49.

Mondeo had been sent to do lots more groups, therapy experiences, some similar to and some different from those available through the Tushita programme for visiting sannyassins and normal healthy neurotics. He was away a lot and so she swept and cleaned and bought stuff: fiery, hot-spiced fabrics for creations made by tailors in the MG road.

Sometimes, Niyati went out in a rickshaw and sat in a juice-bar just off the MG road where the elevation descended, down which slid cart after cart, bullock drawn, and leaking excrement. Inside the same tape played endlessly, the romantic, modal, twang of the latest Bollywood Bonanza. Bench tables, with upholstered parallel seating, served mango-pulp in dusty bowls, cream flecked with speckled grey swirling thinly into the sticky orange paste. She'd eat the pulp in small spoonfuls, taken from the side of the bowl, saving the cream for last, an inversion of winter porridge catching the melting gold-top-top before it discoloured and disappeared into the grey gruel. She'd pass the time smoking a beedie, trying to be serene. She reckoned that mango pulp was about 300 calories. Blessed dysentery came, went and returned and, little by little, the youthful bloom of happy middle-class chops and mash gave way to a drawn and restless look.

Outside, and she never went far, beyond the flimsy leather-topped bamboo screen that separated the juice bar from real life, the detritus flowed up and down the yellowing street: bullocks, legs spattered red with kicked-up Diwali dyes, chipping blue and white painted horns, tired bells around their necks; curled sticks, like horns, flicking in small boys' hands to hurry their slow passing; beggars, lone and scrawny; worn, tattered women in saris, torn, green, purple, what Auntie Vi would call mauve; men, leering, young, old, deformed; children, working for rice; and the man on the trolley was there, no legs, one arm, big lips wherever she went, a huge head on a missing body.

Niyati was frightened and the shopkeepers knew it. Scratching at a life. Next to the biscuit shop, which had a counter and a proper glass-fronted display cabinet, a stall sold gin, illicitly poured into sauce bottles under the counter. The alcoholic homeless mirrored a Hogarth she'd studied for Art A level; eighteenth century imperialism.

She went from the broad-fronted fabric palaces to the open shutter, let down forwards to create a table in front of the window, of a chemist's shop. Norrinyl 1: the pill. Six packets for 12 rupees. It was printed on the side of the packet. The chemist turned his lip up and shook his arm to show his chunky gold watch and link strap to the Western Whore.

Pune offered something other. Bhagwan offered time and space, the tantric master yet to mutate to the Bodhidharma of his final years, and so Niyati pottered, tallying days in the hot, Indian acridity, until it was time to return to Tushita, flowing-triumphant and dressed to match yet dreading the unknown and the increasingly depressing awareness that, the more therapy and personal growth she embraced, the more fucked up she became. There seemed no end to the oppression of having to constantly off-load one's own neurosis in a quest for freedom. Thinking of going back, to Tushita's new shutters in the group room, sealed as-if-in-case another hanging child might bolt, left a worm in the pith of her bones. Niyati prepared for another meeting with the master. She and Mondeo had grown quite nonchalant about the washing and the scent-free zones so they washed early but spent the day in the ashram café, reading *Sannyas Magazine*, before going to rest in the afternoon and wash, just once more. She hoped that Bhagwan might help her shake off her neurosis and enter a state of deep let go and, mustering her strength and risking the ridicule of more enlightened sannyassins, she decided to ask about sex. Washed and ironed, Niyati sat before the master.

Bhagwan beamed.

"Hello, Niyati. What about you?"

She stuttered, "I have a sexual problem."

"Tell me."

And she tried.

"I, I. Well, sometimes, every time, nearly all the time, when, when I'm making love I get this very strong feeling to, well, um, stop. I just don't seem to enjoy it much. Not much, well sometimes but then, no. I. I feel there must be something really terribly badly wrong with me." He talked to her about misery. The great corruption was in that lesson that taught us that everything was ok when we were miserable and that we should feel guilty about our pleasures. Sex, he explained, offered an opening, an access route to the goal of the ancient mystics, Samadhi. If the ancients sought to transcend the body, she could experiment with becoming absolutely

85

possessed by, and absolutely possessing of her body, to find the ecstatic transcendence through orgasm and glimpse the divine.

There were three steps. The first, a temporary switch of roles by which she would become the active partner and so less of a spectator in the affair. The second was to create an elaborate crazy ritual of singing, dancing and playing music: a noisy incensed foreplay involving her behaving like a wild and possessed animal. The third thing, he explained, lyrically and magically, concerned the nature of life itself, and the transience of the benediction of life. As she sat there, bathed, she felt the delight in life Bhagwan felt and she felt sure that she could build her temple, starting at the foundations, reaching to the stars with joy and the delight he conveyed.

Niyati smiled. Mondeo beamed but, try as she might, she couldn't feel joyful about him.

The following night, Niyati decided she really should try and dance like a wild animal, as Bhagwan had advised, before ravishing Mondeo. His little catholic eyes lit up as she busied herself with incense, bought and reserved specially for the occasion. As she moved, hanging orange longhis up against the light, Mondeo glowed as if with a UK daytrip suntan. As she made her advance, in ecstatic dance, choosing to remain veiled in an old bikini, catalogue underwear being antithetic to the primeval scene, she could feel the Kundalini energy starting to rise. At first this took the form of powerful and bubbling tummy rumbles and she decided to remain watchful and to throw herself more fully into the dance. This was very difficult without a cassette player (the electricity was off) but she managed it by humming Barry White's *My First, My Last, My Everything*, hoping and praying that Mondeo would be no more her last than he was her first. She closed her eyes and thought back to the sensuous tumble on the leafy compost she had shared with her crush, that Irish-artist-gardener-Patrick in Streatley-on-Thames. The countryside's manurey-composty richness seemed almost to fill the room there in the East and her stomach stirred again. Mondeo, watching her face contort against the peristalsis of Kundalini moved towards her, tugging at the tie-together sides of her old rose-coloured bikini and in a moment of deep let go, Niyati thrust forward, shouting "WHOO WHOO" as in dynamic mediation. Mondeo, stooping now to untangle the knotted threads of her resistant knickers was suddenly thrown backwards, losing his footing as the floor turned to liquid and with the final "WHOO" Niyati shat herself; the long awaited promised cure-all for any podgy Western girl, that dieting nemesis, dysentery, saved her from a fat, fated embrace with the man she should, sooner rather than later, put at a safe distance from further humiliation.

"Oh My God!"

"Wow! It's. It's such a release," said Niyati and, "Fucking hell. I'm so sorry, Mondeo. I'm so very, very sorry Mondeo."

Things grew tense between Niyati and Mondeo but she was too frightened to leave him. Instead, she got ready to return to the West, passing long nights dancing, solitary, wild and alien in the crowds that gathered round musicians to melt into ether, the beat pulsing through her, ecstatic in the meditation hall; all alone. Perhaps returning is always the best bit. Thirty years later she could still remember her parents' warm love and her dramatic, short, hennaed hair.

Before leaving Pune, liberated by a final scent-free darshan, Niyati had taken a rickshaw to an apothecary and chosen the brightest henna from a jar amongst many stuffed with powders, bark, berries and herbs. The apothecary, a small brown man in a small brown coat, had piled the sweet, sticky powder into a loosely glued brown paper bag which she'd later emptied into a vat of water-boiled lemon juice on the stove, on the hot-white-tiled veranda. Mixing and spreading as hot as she could bear, she plastered her head and sat upright in the midday sun to bake. Darkened green water sludged from the overflow at the back of the veranda and onto the lilies, drying at the side of the house, as the dung ran tepid in the hot sun from the shower adaptation in the recessed and canopied shelter she shared with Mondeo. Her hair, bright orange, now matched the dungaree-style long canvas skirt and bib she'd had made to go over the red-silk tabard and flat leather sandals underneath.

Her father, on her return, had smiled the broadest of smiles and everyone was pleased that she was home. She, being young, had expected a tirade about her hair and her way of life, not knowing very much about love. Lamb and onion sauce dispensed in two parental homes, Niyati and Mondeo returned to Tushita to shake a final revolution from their home.

1979

Gavin Machim had made an enquiry about hiring the barn-space at Tushita for a five-day group, the grand finale of his nine-month intensive encounter group. The group, of 20, had met weekly at Conquestadoor on Wednesdays for intensive confrontation and monthly, at the weekend, for 48-hour marathon-encounter groups. The five-day experience would draw things to a close and prepare participants for re-entry. Those who have been on long journeys often experience raw vulnerability when returning, newly awakened, to mainstream existence. Even the Apollo missions found negotiating a safe landing on their return to earth precarious and unpredictable. It was both frightening and humbling to think that Tushita might be entrusted to support those released from Gavin's orbit to land safely and so know the place as if for the first time. Tushita was asked to provide good food, clean toilets and integrity.

Niyati, post jet-lag, got straight on the phone. Amazing. She couldn't believe it. Gavin: the glorious, hunky, sexy, right-on, straight talking, liberated, chain-smoking-Levis-wearing Governor of the UK group scene on the phone, with her.

They washed and scrubbed and bought new foam batons for beating cushions. They checked Avalon's Bang and Olufsen sound-system in the barn group room and lined up The Temptations, Marvin Gaye and Barry White. 'You're my first, my last, my everything' could refer not just to one woman but also to existence itself and, Niyati thought, just quietly, to Gavin Machim if your luck was in. She couldn't sleep the night before the group started and she was up before Dharma. Poor Dharma was still on baking meditation, so she mixed the yeast and sugar, started the dough and they had an early breakfast together, waiting for time to pass and sampling the latest bitter marmalade before they could deliver the day's supplies to the shops.

Slowly, members of the nine-month intensive encounter therapy group started to arrive.

"Hi," said Richard Parkinson, "Richard. Also known as Parkie. 'Richards to Rags.'" He held out his hand. Niyati smiled. It was quite good; the non-sannyassins weren't that right-on about chitchat and truly that was something she'd missed.

"Richards to? Parkie?"

"Sorry. I thought you were. Err."

"I'm Niyati. I live here. I'm the cook for the week. And you're Richard but you were going to explain about Rags and Richards."

"Yeah. Sure." He was terribly middle class. "Yeah. Well, you see, I'm in television and some of the group think I'm a bit like . . ."

"Don't tell me. The real Parkinson."

"Got it in one. Smart girl. Err-and, and Gavin is just about the only guy in the group who is not called Richard. I mean, Gavin, he's different anyway, 'cause he's in charge and not really one of us. And then, Rags, well, let's put it this way. We were pretty fucked up when we started and we tried to hide the raggy bits of ourselves, so we'll all be proud rags when we leave. Oh, and, yeah! It is quite expensive too."

"What about the women?"

"Yeah. We've got some right little ravers in our party." Chitchat lost its appeal.

More came. Richard, Richard, Richard and Richard were all in something corporate or other and they all wore jeans like Gavin's. They seemed to see self-discovery a bit like Niyati's mum used to view a night at the theatre. They'd paid for it and they expected something to happen to them. Niyati sneered. She lived in Tushita Therapy Commune. Officer class.

Eventually, Gavin turned up driving a Hillman Minx and clearly he'd had a very difficult journey. Road-works, bad directions, (her fault, she blushed) over-heating, (the car and Gavin too by the look) but finally he had arrived. She put the kettle on. The rest of her commune had disappeared. Some were still working at the local hospital, others just didn't seem to care and Mondeo was at the end of the garden fucking about with the asparagus bed. But she got everything wrong. The tea was too strong then not milky enough; then she gave Gavin the sugar but he said that if she cared she'd have added it for him. She was grief-torn yet relieved when he took his Richards and the poor beleaguered women who had come with them off to the group until lunch. It was eerily silent. What sort of group could this be?

The ordeal continued. It was a bit like cooking for Bhagwan. There was no problem with the group. They'd eat just about anything and they had to. Tushita became famous for its brown rice and parsnips as much as for bread and marmalade but Gavin had to be treated with special care.

Retreating upstairs he expected his meals on a tray and things had to be just so. She got the hang of the cups of tea because he drank a lot of those but his other sensitivities ranged unpredictably. But nothing was too much trouble and still she blushed when he thanked her so nicely.

Sunami and Whayve, from the Leeds centre, were still not back from Pune. A couple of Tushitans had gone to help the sannyassins in Leeds who were struggling to get people to work for the meditation centre. This meant there was an empty room at Tushita. Restless, she crept along the passage, stealing from Mondeo's bed and she spent the nights of Gavin's group alone.

One day they went to the river, a conglomerate melee of Tushita residents and Gavin's groupies. Streatley-on-Thames and Gibbs' boat hire. Six canoes on the river and she knew the place well. Choosing the widest but safest part of the river, just above the weir, the lock and the infamous Swan Hotel, they moored and laid out a picnic but Niyati had no appetite. As Gavin tried to serve himself, she leapt, dropping her robe, bikini beneath and diving deep into the muddy-green she swam underwater to the middle of the river. Flip. Back crawl, puppy fat forgotten, Gavin now was on his feet. Stripped to a small, dark, stripe of jockey, he belly flop-skinnied towards her and started to panic. Swimming wasn't his thing. She turned from the opposite bank, cutting through the water to catch him. Treading water. Trading pride for care. Later, packing up, he trailed after them, stooping to stuff the top of her bikini into the back pocket of his jeans.

Niyati rinsed her bikini-bottoms under the mixer tap in the tiny scullery and scrabbled in the picnic basket, looking for the other half.

"G'day," Gavin's twang. "You'll be looking for this." He dropped a river-stained bikini-bra into the sink. She blushed.

"Oh. Thank you. Where did you?"

"Oh come on, lady. Don't play games with me."

"What d'you mean?"

"Oh! Oh!" he put both hands against his cheeks in pantomime horror, squeaking, "Oh Gavin. I've lost my bikini. Oh, dear. Oh, no!" he scowled but then he slapped her, roundly, on the arse. "Check yer, later, Hen." Glaswegian ghetto speak.

Mondeo was sneezing. He'd had to go to Leamington Spa to see an acupuncturist about his eczema, anal fissures and hay fever. He pulled into the drive in the tangerine 2CV and wearily lowered the fold-open windows shut. He climbed out and opened the boot, dragging to his feet a huge sack of stone ground flour and another of preserving sugar from the bakery in South Moreton; clearly Tushita posed no threat to those dealing in bread or marmalade. Niyati, bikini dangling from her wrist, stroked him lightly on the arm, feeling the rough hairs, the sandpaper rash, the catholicism seeping.

"I've made a great big jug of lemonade. Just lemons, water and sugar-cane juice, if you want some. Shall I bring some through to the snug for you? It's sealed against the pollen, there."

"I can't drink anything except spring water. Sham's put me on an alpha diet. Got to avoid acids, Niyati." She scoffed.

"Fucking crap. You paid £12 for a fucking ego massage." He made her cringe now, his eyes red-rimmed under thick eyebrows, square gold-rimmed spectacles. Anyone else would wear glasses. A small man, wearing Thai Chi shoes and a business shirt, undone, tapped her on the arm. One of Gavin's Richards. He needed to phone London. His office was bidding for a franchise. She took him to the phone-box in the hall.

"You can ask them to phone you back," Niyati

explained, smiling. "It's just - we've had a few challenges with communication. People taking the piss, you know?"

Richard pulled out a filo-fax and started hunting for his P.A's home number. Mondeo slunk past into the snug, a copy of *The Observer* secreted under a loose-weave amber shawl. Niyati moved along the corridor, past racks of orange coats and out again to the summer sun and the washing line. She reached, pegging the bikini, exposing a young filly's legs. Gavin whistled from the barn door. Slowly, slowly, catch your monkey.

There was a problem. Although Gavin's professional ethics prevented him from dating participants of his groups, there was still Khuntarina, a strapping girl who'd come to Tushita for a marathon and never left, taking sannyas – writing away for a mala and a name, which had only just arrived. She was slightly in awe of Niyati and single but surely too large. She'd taken to helping in the kitchen and Gavin was faced with a choice. The two girls competed for his cups of tea, Khuntarina providing the lion's share as the group drew to a close. There was music and dancing, wine even. The groupies were being born to the new world, the nine-month encounter's end their new beginning. Gavin sat on a bursting Habitat floor cushion, smoking. Niyati seized her prey.

"Dance?"

"Yer-on."

She did the sannyassin shuffle, an adaptation of the dynamic meditation. She'd first done the dynamic in that fatal marathon encounter group, with Gavin looking on. Ten minutes' fierce breathing through the nose; ten minutes' catharsis, killing your mother, screaming out primal rage or whatever; ten minutes' pelvic thrusting, shouting 'whoo, whoo, whoo' from deep within the sex centre, the lower chakra on the quickening exhalation; and finally ten minutes spent stock still, feeling that higher vibration. Dancing, then, needed to demonstrate equal bio-energetic fluidity to prove that you weren't fucked up. Gavin, probably more of a complainer than a demonstrator, was soon ready for another cup of tea and they sneaked away together to the kitchen dark-deserted. Khuntarina (big-girl) and Mondeo were both away to bed, anticipating an early morning rising having offered Dharma a day's grace from the bread.

Gavin stared into her eyes and she flinched. He had eyelashes where they shouldn't have been, right up to the corners of his eyes.

"You look like you've seen a ghost," he said and she hid her shock. She was unaccustomed to covering things up and she started to breathe too quickly, in case he could detect a lie.

"No, no ghosts. It's your eyes. They're, like, I don't know. I think I've seen them somewhere before. Like Bhagwan's, perhaps."

"Yeah, baby. All the better to eat you with. Fancy a walk? It's kind of uncomfortable here, for me, you know? I'm still at work, your man's around here some place."

"Don't worry about him. What do you mean, working? Do you see running groups as working?"

"Man." They wandered, up and down the garden path, past the bikini on the line. "The offending article," said he.

"What?"

"The bikini. You laid a trail. A sign. I wouldn't have known, otherwise."

"I didn't. Known what? Who to choose?"

"Easy, girl. There was never a contest, you know that. Just play. Just play." He kissed her. Long, lithe tongue. Hot. Her mouth completely at home in his. The whole house was packed. A Richard and a rag were rumbled in her spare-bed;

the barn full, they found a car with a bench-seat-back and fell into the show-off sex of the day. Unabridged, unbridled, suck it and see.

"Run away with me!" he said.

"Where?"

"Milton Keynes; it's not built yet."

"Where?"

"Newport Pagnell. Just off the M1." She'd never heard of either but she packed a bag, a trunk, her *Sannyas* magazines, teddy and her letters from Bhagwan as she cried.

"Mondeo. I. . . I. . . Will I ever see you again? I. . ."

"Niyati. We're sannyassins," said Mondeo, sticky with dough, "We have to let go of time, possession. Go."

Everyone was shocked. A blur of orange-huggers stood at the door, waiting for marmalade buns, as she held Gavin's bonnet open and he hot-wired the Hillman Minx.

"Lost the key, Hen."

1979

II

Gavin's house seemed austere and frighteningly magnolia. Expanses of wall, broken only by shotguns hanging horizontally, displayed his newfound fascination with country life.

"What d'you reckon?" he asked, moving from the post, piled neatly on the table, to the kettle just the other side of the terrace's long front room.

"It looks lonely," Niyati said, wanting life with Gavin to be like a group.

He had listened to her then and she had known that what she said was as true as she knew it to be. They'd been to a builder's merchant in a small town down the road, taking a lurcher-dog with them in the back of the car. Two children would arrive days later, fresh from a seaside break with their mother, someone Niyati didn't yet know.

They painted bright, white emulsion and sunshine-yellow gloss as the washing line shone with the colours of the rising sun. Gavin sent off for a new name in the post and bleached all his denim, which she dyed with Tangerine, Ochre and Vermillion wash-in-dye. Neighbours peered over their parallel rows of runner beans, tall, to gawp at the lines of stiffening cotton, reaching up and down the 180 foot stretch of narrow terraced garden. Narrow-boat gypsies jeered as they walked the tow-path with the dog and she tasted, for the first time, middle England's make-do for the Thames.

"You can't swim in this, Doll."

All night they talked as she tried to orient to a new existence. All day they made love in the fields, skylarks higher than it was possible to fly, roughshod ramblers turning a blind eye. It was *Cider with Rosie*, heaven on earth.

He cut her a key and she felt the delight of knowing that no one would shout if she didn't wash her cup and they found lots of money in a box.

She'd wake before him in the morning and walk through the village to the shop. The grumpy post-master didn't speak on the third day but handed her 20 Dunhill International and 40 Players Navy Cut with her loaf. She made sandwiches and a flask of tea and ferried washing out and in; waiting, anxious, waiting.

The night before the kids returned, he said something rather strange.

"Let's have an ordinary night tonight."

"What do you mean? How can a night be ordinary when we are so in love?"

"Yeah. Well you know what I think about that, huh? Illusions, sweet illusions. I'm a few years ahead of you, girl. You know. This is good, don't get me wrong, now, but I need a bit of space." A lot of people had found her boundless, puppy-like energy sometimes hard to take. Premda had told her that her courage and openness could be quite hard to be with while staying centred. She eased.

"Ok. Gavin. Oh, I wonder what your new name will be. Um. What's an ordinary night mean, then, my love?"

"Bit of telly. Smoke some dope."

"Dope?" she was horrified. This was Gavin Machim, an ex-trainee of Vamoosh's, the addiction therapist. Ok, so Vamoosh smoked but that was kind of ok because he was just so close to enlightenment she expected he just did that to press people's buttons and set them free from their repressions, conditioning and neuroses. But, Gavin? She had to say 'yes', that was one thing she had learnt; that when she was experiencing resistance she should allow herself to say yes and watch, be a witness as existence taught her a lesson.

Gavin pulled a small, portable television, black and white, from the cupboard under the stairs.

"Right. I'm going to have to balance this fucking thing on the armchair. Are you going to keep wriggling? Huh? Because this fucking box moves out of focus if you shake the floor."

"No. It's ok. I'll just sit here. You want some tea?"

"Yeah. Ok. You make the tea. Get the biscuits. I'll skin up." She did as she was told and sat with five bourbons and a powder blue straight up and down pottery mug balanced on the arm of the sofa under the bay window. He stared at the screen while they smoked, not speaking, not touching, nothing at all.

She was rigid. Her foot had gone numb but she didn't dare move. The phone rang and he ignored it as she sat and traced her parents lost inside; her father's proud smile; her mother's zebra sun dress with the matching jacket, wide stripes dangling over the campsite stove in Italy. Ponderous hot tears ran down her cheeks. She knew that dope could make you feel things more strongly and heighten consciousness and as she thought so, she stared at the top if his head. The more she looked, the more she could see he had spaced out. She knew this was a really bad thing. Just after her first marathon, she'd gone for a drink with Premda, then Derek, in Wallingford, to The George and he'd woken her from a dream.

"Spacing out."

"What?"

"You're spacing out. I've been watching you. What's going on?"

"Well, I'm just watching the people. Those two over there, Derek. Do you think they're married or brother and sister?" Premda had confronted her quite sternly and reminded her that every minute of every day she should be self-conscious rather than spaced out focussing on others. It had been a tough lesson, she liked people watching, but one she'd been grateful to learn.

As she sat, on the sofa, not moving, she remembered the technique Mondeo had learned from the Vipassana group in Pune. It was one adapted from Zen, used by the monks. Monks paced lines of meditators, noting which were watching the breath and which were not. Those who'd spaced out received a blessing; a short, sharp tap on the back of the head with a stick. Next to her, on the sofa, a fly swat. In a flash, she knew what to do to save the situation. She lifted the swat, high above her head and slowly lowered it to hold it poised and inches above the back of Gavin's head as he sat on the floor at her feet. Suddenly, Zen-like and in a moment of total focus she brought the fly swat down, hard, with a sharp crack and it hit Gavin fair and square in the middle of his bald patch.

"Wake up. Wake up!" she shouted. "You're spacing out! Beware!" She was certain he'd know what she meant.

Thunder cracked. The television leapt from the

armchair, completely out of focus as it splattered and fizzled on the hard pine floor. Gavin turned and raged, tearing the cover from the sofa she sat on, hurling her cup that shattered in confetti-like shards, trailing brown sticky tea into the bright, light Dulux paint. He roared and he bellowed, all trace of Puerto Rican American absent.

"You fucking bitch, you stupid fucking cow. Who the fuck do you think you are? You arrogant fucking controlling fucking bitch. Get the fuck out of my sight you fucking twat-faced cunt." Glaswegian language, actions to match, he grabbed a pine dining chair and held it menacingly above his head, bringing it down on the matching pine table, shattering it into six. He swung and pulled the door open. "You better get up them fucking stairs. No fucking body touches me. You get that? You don't fucking mess with me you fucking hear me?"

"Gavin, I was just trying to wake you up." He was not listening. He grabbed the back of her robe, a hessian caftan, pride of her MG road expeditions, with a long hood hanging pointed down her back. As he pulled, the neck tightened round her throat and she found herself on the fourth stair, slumped and bruised. She crept away, bedroom, bathroom, under the covers. Sweating.

Downstairs, the storm continued. A plant. A clock. A large Nescafe storage jar of sugar cast from the back of the kitchen to shatter, missing the window, hitting the stereo and grinding into the turntable, the back of the cupboard, the folds of the sofa. The dog whined at the back door and as wood cracked, hard against the wall she knew he'd gone, taking the dog, letterbox banging in the aftermath, leaving her not knowing when he'd return. She crept to the bottom stair, pushed the door, surveyed the scene and, clasping her mala with Bhagwan's locket, thankfully still fully strung and intact, she climbed the stairs and buried herself in bedclothes, waiting for morning.

It was hard to unravel the story. They barely spoke as they buried the debris the next day, baking cakes before the kids returned. The main thing was she knew it was her fault.

The mother returned the children, Megan, 7, and Ben, 18 months. They looked her up and down.

"She's pretty," said Megan as she clambered up the shelves of the cupboard under the stairs to find Ben a bottle and some apple juice. Later, Ben climbed into bed and wriggled between them. These two were the centre of Gavin's world and Niyati struggled to learn the child-centred approach, which might well have served Saffron and Scarlet, commune kids, better than communal neglect.

Two days later, when his new name, Swami Prem Novino arrived, he changed its intonation so that Novino, pronounced in Glaswegian, sounded more like 'never-know' than the staccato of a Hindi 'vino'. He was miffed to be thought a Prem, word on the street being that Bhagwan named you Prem something or other if you were more like the acceptors, as she was, who dashed across the road of life without looking, than the hard-nosed rejectors who weighed things up with care as he did and were usually given the prefix, Anand. Prem was, he thought, for poofs.

Novino asked the children's mother, Helga, to tea and sat hugging her fondly, singing along to Carly Simon, telling Helga the mother and Niyati that it was blissful to be with the two women he loved, both at once.

Niyati felt sometimes that this life, in terraced housing, was more challenging than the commune life she had abandoned just for love.

She found the quiet mornings interrupted, Novino and the

kids beating her to the kitchen table, waiting, a nation of three, the breakfast committee. Nothing she cooked suited their tastes and Navino explained she had a lot to learn. The television and the dope stood in for conversation late at night and the rigid pose on the sofa, to keep the box in focus, put a strain on the relationship. She didn't know any of the songs he knew and she was utterly ashamed when the washing machine, after 23 years of loyal service, gave up the ghost when she stuffed it with an optimistically heavy bucket of nappies. The money in the box ran out and orange lost its appeal.

Helga the mother, who was too busy studying childhood trauma to keep the kids full-time, took them away for a day and a night and Niyati looked forward to some more of the good times she and Novino had shared, three weeks before. On her way downstairs, she heard Novino on the phone:

"Hello," she overheard. "Yeah. Hi there Miah. It's Gavin here. No, no, no. Fuck that Novino shit. I'm not wearing a fucking necklace. It's Gavin, sweetheart, Gavin."

Niyati's heart hurt. Had he not read the beautiful letter Bhagwan Shree had sent: 'now use only the beautiful new name Bhagwan Shree has given and drop identification with the past'? She'd have to be brave. She ran back upstairs to catch her breath, to centre herself. She hadn't done dynamic mediation since she'd left Tushita. She'd been worried about it, really. She tried to focus on her higher energies before she confronted Gavin with himself.

Later, tears, a small palm, its stem torn in two, earthen-pot muddying the carpet, two threats and her love dismissed, she boarded an Oxford bus to find her way back to Tushita.

The Tushita reception committee were all guns blazing. It didn't go too well. The commune, in just three weeks, had rearranged its ranks, large Khuntarina on Mondeo's arm, his eczema quickly fading. Niyati shivered in the barn, unwelcome. In her bag she found a huge Cadbury's dairy milk bar which she had intended to melt over vanilla ice-cream for Gavin's kids. She allowed herself eight squares before sleeping and another eight when she woke, staring at the Bang and Olufsen system Avalon had left behind and which had replaced the Sony stacking stereo, contemplating her fate.

The options were not great. She could, at a pinch, have gone back to mum and dad but the thought of living with people who, unaware as they were, had no interest in personal growth, was anathema to her. She had heard that sannyassins who worked for Khatahpult, the meditation centre in London which had sent them Avalon and Sacharina, would offer payment for bus fares and food to those who surrendered to work meditation there but still there remained the problem of where to live. The only option that Niyati could come up with, for now, was staying put in the barn, to wait and see what might happen next. Exhausted from her ordeal, she fell asleep under a rough and discarded, dark blue and pale blue reversible, polyester sleeping bag.

A cockerel. A car. Then,

"Fucking heap of shit." A car door slammed and Niyati heard the crunch of gravel as footsteps moved away from the barn towards the house. Five minutes passed.

"You can take yourself away, Gavin, if you please." Mondeo, terse, tense, but, did she hear him right? Was he addressing Gavin?

"In the fucking Barn, Gav." More sharp footsteps as Mondeo swung towards the house, banging the door behind him. He was never very good in the morning. Niyati huddled under the blue cloud and the barn door let in patchy, dusty light, framing Gavin's form. She coughed.

"I didn't see you there Doll. Come to me. Come to me.

There. Let it go, my sweet. Let it go. Yeah. Yeah. You need love. Good girl. Yeah." He lit two Players Navy Cut and passed her one. Niyati couldn't believe it. He did care. He did. He had driven, all of 49 miles, through the by-roads and side roads that connected Milton Keynes to Oxfordshire, in a Hilman Minx without a key, practically through the night, just for her. She fell into his arms. "And this time, my love, we're not letting those fucking sannyassins intimidate us into going without what's rightly yours, right?"

Niyati had never felt so supported in her life; the future spread before her like an undrawn canvas and, with Gavin's help, she collected her Brabantia knives and her Le Creuset set from the kitchen, generous presents for life from Auntie Vi for her 21st, while the commune convened in the group room. She and Gavin sped off into the unknown, back to Milton Keynes. The commune, too late to stop them hotwiring the car, shook its fist through the group room window.

1977

III

When she'd been back with him again for a week, Gavin found Niyati a bicycle. She had been out, to London, to see what the people there thought about starting a meditation centre in Milton Keynes. Hitching back down the M1 and making the journey alone round the lake from Newport Pagnell services, she arrived to find all the lights out and just a torch seeming to stand guard, atop the kitchen table. As she pushed the front door, it opened and, carefully moving forwards, she saw the internal door was open too and there, on the table, with a ribbon and its front light, shining brightly, was a midwife's bike, painted silver. Gavin, Ben and Megan suddenly leapt from the pantry,

"Surprise! Surprise!" and Niyati really felt one of the family. Now they could ride together and she would be able to keep up on a proper ladies' bike. But autumn hung gloomily around the nightly vigils over the sensitive television, which could not be nudged or jolted and Niyati's boundless love retreated behind a nameless fear.

Two needs grew. Although Niyati was in awe of Gavin's tidy group of intimate friends, she craved sannyassin company. Gavin, having run short of Marathon Encounters to conduct, impressed upon her, daily, the need for her to contribute financially and beyond taking care of his needs.

"We're talking spondoolics, Niyats. Hard cash, girl."

Niyati, killing two birds with one stone, found that if she used her bike for the first leg of her journey, she could cover train fares and cigarettes with what she could earn from commuting to Khatahpult in London to offer guidance and administration to the swell of incoming seekers. Yet, increasingly as the nights drew in, she found on her return that Gavin had already fired up the touchy TV, and she found it easiest to creep up to bed alone, lest she upset the apparatus and her Love.

From time to time, on Fridays, she might meet Gavin in London after work since he ran sessions there in a private clinic for very unhealthy people who needed intensive, one to one guidance and pillow bashing to help them manage unexpressed pain. On these nights they'd walk with rapid steps, hardly speaking, to stand and shiver at Brent Cross, waiting for the coach to Milton Keynes. Invariably they'd stop off in Bletchley for several joints and some Mars Bars with a dear man, Jeremy Moss, famous for being the first employee of the Open University. These were playful, happy times, without the threat of temperamental televisions or an arduous encounter with the children's mother. One night in dead of winter they'd sledged from top to bottom of the gravel pit, Gavin on a sledge of his own, Niyati lying on top of Jeremy as he lay on top of his. Reaching the end of a fabulous run she'd found Jeremy had lost their sledge at the top of the hill and she'd travelled the distance comfortably on top of him while he had had only the protection of his now button-less donkey-jacket between the slope and him. Another night they became graffiti revolutionaries, painting anarchist symbols in red on bill-boards and hoardings, giggling with mirth at these armchair activists' nights on the tiles. But returning, to the dour, dark drudgery of living on scraps of love, cut through Niyati's youth like a knife.

Inevitably, as Christmas drew near, the unsustainable collapsed in yet another red-blooded fury of Gavin's followed by its close relation, the two week spell in Coventry for Niyati until, eventually, Gavin had to call in his friends.

Since Niyati's first eviction from Gavin's life, and the night spent with no future beyond the blue sleeping bag in the barn, she had been a little bit more canny about back-up plans. While working for Khatahpult, Niyati had also been busy networking and had made friends with a community of sannyassins who were squatting at the time in a huge house in Islington. She was ready for Gavin's friends.

Rosemary and Carl, who had been married but weren't any longer came along with Rosemary's man, Mark Weatherby, from the marathons. Carl's Marie who had once been Mark's came too; Helga, Gavin's wife-cum-mother-of-the-children and best friend, together with her boyfriend, (who had converted from George to Jeremiah following a past-life experience in which he had discovered he and Helga had lived as shepherds in 1645) and her girlfriend who was also her boyfriend's girlfriend, were invited round to help Niyati decide what to do.

All Gavin's friends were trained therapists with exceptional skills when it came to interpersonal relationships. This was evident in that, although nearly everyone had slept with or was still sleeping with nearly everyone else, and there was potential for all kinds of power trips and collusion, these people navigated without fear and could therefore say a lot of positive things, authentically. They had done so much therapy (called 'work') that, with the exception of Gavin's secret rages, there was no indication of repressed anger or neurosis. Niyati felt absolutely inadequate in their presence since, living with a therapist, she had learnt that she had probably got to spend longer in therapy than the length of her life to date before she could even hope to have shaken off the terrors and neuroses inevitably derived from a comfortable middle-class upbringing. At least these people had, with only perhaps two notable exceptions, been dragged up by real people with real feelings and no money, abusive as that might have made them. Once the therapists had worked through their anger about being beaten by alcoholic fathers or unfeeling mothers, they were suitably equipped to support others through their similar pain. But Niyati had further to go.

Jeremiah, Helga's boyfriend and Helga's girlfriend's boyfriend, had offered a synopsis of Niyati's case, hovering as a kettle boiled. He seemed to be equipped to give an overview of almost anything.

"I don't think you'll find, Niyati, that your primal pain, backed-up shit if you would like to call it that, is going to be the most problematic of your issues. I know that at Tushita, as is only right for beginners in therapy, you did a lot of screaming and beating cushions. And in India Bhagwan suggested you had a rest. Yes? Perhaps it is really a waste of time but let's see. Now, I'm not suggesting that your elemental feelings must not be brought to the fore. Not at all. You will have to go in quite deep though. And even then, once you've mastered the breathing and diaphragmatic movement required to scream and beat a cushion, you must decide what it is you want to scream. And this is where your difficulties lie. You have to locate your feelings in the first place and of course, you can't. Why?"

Jeremiah was a university lecturer, used to giving hour-long talks. He was, as well, a humanistic therapist working towards the liberation of human potential. Thus he was a bit long-winded yet he had integrated his experiential learning seamlessly with academia and was so congruent that he talked only in the language of wholeness. His monologues held most people enraptured. He went on.

"The problem I think you face is one of linguistic conditioning. I have been monitoring you quite closely and I have noticed that although you are able to use the language of the emotions, this is laid atop a sinister and impenetrable web of automatic, conditioned responses. Take, for example, when we arrived just now. I asked you, 'How are you?' and, without a moment's reflection I got, 'Very well thank you. How are you?' Of course, you are clearly not very well and you have little interest in me. In terms of the overlaying of therapeutic terminology, you might say, 'I can't get my head round that' to suggest you understand you need to distinguish your thoughts from your feelings rather than feeling your thoughts are actually you; and sometimes you say, 'My sense is that I was pretty much ok as a child' but really, if you look again, you have no idea where your head divides from your heart or how much, or how ok the thing is that you sense, or what you sense at all and it's all just one mighty big mind-fuck. A construction of meaningless words."

Jeremiah paused and Niyati felt pretty stuck. She couldn't speak, because that would involve proving his point since she had nothing to choose from but the words in her head. So she raised her left eyebrow, in miniscule. Acknowledged, he went on:

"I wonder, can you understand, the impact of such counter-intuitive programming? I think it unlikely you will ever even be able to identify the feelings you are having. So, the expression of your feelings is not really the issue. Your problem is you don't know what they are. In fact, I wonder if you've got any." Niyati had appreciated for some time that the more underhand methods her parents had used to keep her in order, such as the withdrawal of pocket money or an insistence she complete her homework before going out, would take years to unpick. Such self-knowledge had, in part, informed Niyati's decision to put out a few feelers about places to stay in London. The added complication of her linguistic handicap seemed to imply that she had little hope of ever managing to overcome the neurosis of 'coming out sideways' rather than saying exactly what she meant or how she felt because she could never know. It made perfect sense; if she didn't have a language for it, how could she possibly know what to feel? Or should that be the other way round? She was lost. She must have been more than a little irritating to live with: in Glaswegian, a pain in the arse.

It was humiliating to feel so exposed and to feel the friendship of these people slipping away. After all, as far as anyone was prepared to admit, Gavin had never before been pushed to loosen the boundaries of self-control and act out his anger on people and things. She struggled to accommodate this new self-knowledge in a framework which had run out of time:

"Oh," she gasped, "I understand. It's Orwellian really."

"Oh for Christ's sake," said Rosemary.

"Bear with me. Orwell's *Nineteen Eighty Four* forwards the view that through dumbing down language and restricting what people are able to say, they will be less trouble. They will be unable to detect their oppression and so might submit to it more readily. Is that what you mean? Have I been talked out of ever becoming a normal healthy neurotic? Or surely, that must work the other way round too. If you take away my expressions, the language I have used since birth, and give me new words of your choosing rather than mine, won't that be kitting me up to express your feelings rather than my own?"

"That's a mind-fuck," explained Helga the mother.

Niyati poured water into a tea-pot.

After everyone had made sure they had a cup of tea and that there would be an ashtray in easy reach once they sat down, they started with a group hug and then Helga, (who was also Gavin's wife and Jeremiah's girlfriend's girlfriend and so Jeremiah's girlfriend too - to save on rent – meaning that Gavin and Niyati were passive partners in the extended family web and so subject to both Jeremiah's and Helga's edicts), suggested they initiate proceedings by sharing an affirmation for Niyati to make her feel ok since really they were Gavin's friends not hers. Helga then said that she hadn't really meant that and that they were her friends. Niyati had to forget all about Hidden Agendas, Linguistic Handicaps and Freudian Slips in order to keep up with the gist of what was going on. She deduced that the meeting had been called because Gavin had found her very difficult to tolerate but she hadn't expected everyone to come armed with so much information. Niyati felt awkward about going on at all with, evidently, no hope.

The affirmations, which in general concerned her youthful optimism, dispensed, they sat down and Gavin took the floor.

"You guys, here. You know me, right? I'm a family man, yeah? And nothing matters to me more than my kids, yeah?" Helga, his kids' mother made a sweet sort of 'ah' sound and, sitting next to Gavin of course, she gently stroked his back. Gavin, buoyed up, went on,

"And, this girl here. Niyati, jewel. You know, you're

112

lovely, sweet, well- meaning and the kids like her, I mean you, yeah, they like you, If you don't know what I think of you in the sack, well. I'm not going to tell you. but you know what?" and his tone was on the turn, "You just gotta be after my fuckin approval all the fucking long day long and I just wanna go, you know what? Go, fuckin hang it on the wall? Yeah? You know what I'm sayin', yeah? Now, you can work this one out; you're bright. I'm just out of a long-term relationship and I have my priorities here with the kids. Beyond that, I don't have much space for something that isn't going too well. I can't be chasing around at the end of every day telling you that everything is ok. Right? You gotta get that sorted out, girl, and you know the only person that's gonna be able to sort it? We're talking about whose responsibility that is? Huh? Yeah. That's right. Yeah." The crooner returned seeing her submission gently rolling down her face: hot, childish, lost, hopeless tears. Marie rushed to her side with the tissues, trying to help,

"You remember, Carl. How you used to say the same to me? That I was looking for approval?" Carl, a psychologist from the Open University with an interest in meditation, looked totally shocked.

"Well, no, my lovely, no. I don't think you should be so hard on yourself. You know, it was me. I needed to adjust. I'd been used to having it all my own way, like. I needed to, you know. Learn to live and let live, you know honey?" Helga was straight in there, on cue it seemed,

"But Gavin's helping here, Carl, he's helping Niyati to live, here, Carl, to let go of this need for reassurance." Helga, having been married to Gavin herself continued, "You know, just supposing this needy-clingy thing that Niyati does, here. Just supposing that were to press Gavin's buttons. Well, Niyati. You see. I've been working with this couple." Helga, too, dedicated her time to working one to one with fucked up people for quite-a-lot-an-hour. "She, the wife, came to me first; she wanted him to stop drinking and having violent rages. But you know what? We had to get together, the two of them and me, for quite a few sessions, about 12, until, finally, the wife was ready to ask herself what it was she was doing to make her husband drink and act out violently. You get what I'm saying? A relationship, it so easily polarises so that somebody feels hard done by; and that is such an easy place to be because you can just sit there blaming the other person for being a bully or not giving you what you need. You have to take responsibility for yourself here. That's a big responsibility. You've got to ask yourself what you are doing to make Gavin unhappy."

"Why shouldn't the poor girl have a bit of reassurance?" went on Carl. But Niyati couldn't listen.

"No, Carl. It's alright. Sorry. I'm alright. Gavin's right, you know? Helga's hit the nail on the head there. I have to take responsibility for myself here, Carl, because I am not a girl. I'm a woman, right? And a woman stands on her own two feet and knows her own worth right?" Mark Weatherby liked this and as he twirled his keys on a long embroidered ribbon, he had the air of a cheer leader at an American baseball match.

"Wow. Niyati. Brave words, girl. Woman, sorry. Woman." Gavin picked up a thread.

"So, you're ok with that, Niyati, yeah? You're gonna give me my space back, take off into the unknown, go see if you can't get yourself sorted out? Yeah? That's my girl? Yeah, I know. I know." Niyati had clearly missed a bit of the conversation at some point but, assuming she must have been spacing out, or mind-fucking, she let it go. Gavin delineated his view of her future. "Yeah. Here, here. Doesn't mean we can't, you know, we can carry on, when I'm free, you know, get together when the wind blows. You just gotta do a bit of work on yourself, find yourself somewhere to put roots down. Find out who you are. You get it? Ok. Ok. Here. Here. Marie, pass that box, eh? Tissues. Marie. Wake up for fuck's sake." Marie was frowning at Gavin then searching Carl's face for a clue. She shoved the tissues across the table. "Thanks. There."

The deal was sealed as the loving professionals drew close for an intense group hug which left one of Niyati's arms, dangling about on the periphery, a spare part.

In a week, by Friday, she had taken her last and final small bag of clothes with her to work her fifth shift of the week at Khatahpult. As she added that sad piece of luggage to the pile behind her desk, she surveyed all that she might take with her to her future and thought it might slot in very well with life in an Islington squat. Really, those posh pans and the knives? It was a pity about the bike, which he'd told her to leave at the station. Who needed to carry such things through life?

1980

Khatahpult, which had heating and some friendly faces, sustained Niyati. She dated Gavin, but only when he came to town. Crumbs thrown on the hard ground. January, after a bitter, soulless Christmas, had found her in a Hackney council flat, signing a weekly rent book with the name Gerry Rosenburg. The sannyassins she had been living with had been re-housed when Islington Council had decided to demolish their squat. Gerry, offered a flat of his own, didn't need the space. She shared with Semoline and Scrambolina, he a poverty consciousness awareness counsellor, she a whole-food chef who danced for a peep show overnight to make up the rent. Their paths rarely crossed.

The first surprise was the winter without parents or a commune to keep her warm. Although boarded up and waiting for proper double-glazing, the windows gave no shelter. In February, wrapped in every orange cloth that she could find, she shivered on the overground train, a bus, a train and a walk to Streatley where her father bought two shelves with brackets and drove her back to Hackney straightaway. He drilled and kept his mouth shut, leaving a fan heater and his love.

It was all very good.

Although Khatahpult Meditation Centre was the first UK centre, Tushita being the second, this first was not a commune. Khatahpult was right at the top of a warehouse; one floor housed a sweatshop and, on the floor beneath those who came and went from meditations, a sausage factory chopped carcasses. Sometimes you'd find a trotter or an eye in the lift. Niyati's job was now to lead meditations, plan groups and do the accounts. They paid her just enough to live and there were perks.

Her standing amongst sannyassins remained high, partly through her association with those in the upper echelons such as Vamoosh and Gavin and partly through her careful exploitation of her reputation for taking risks. Although she felt that intrinsically she was still the puppy-fatted, immature puke Miah had identified in her first marathon, she had managed to drop identification with herself and instead mirrored and imitated those she admired. On a warm day she'd be Vamoosh, on a miserably wet one Amiya, and when she felt invisible she reproduced Gavin's rhetoric. This armoury of self-exploration techniques put her first in line for freebies and special treats if ever any were on offer at Khatahpult. And the jollies of the corporate world were not a patch on the currency of the meditation business.

There were charismatic figures among those closest to Bhagwan, who travelled the world dispensing therapies. Without fail, they passed through Khatahpult. Amongst them were Bioenergetics specialists, Rolfers, Gestaltists, Marathon Encounter leaders, Enlightenment Intensive Masters and those who couldn't quite be categorised, such as Swami Deva Teeteryngh. Teeteryngh's groups involved working with cosmic energy, largely contained within the aura, and confrontational techniques. For example, Teeteryngh might spend some time with eyes closed, tuning in to the sensitive energies around a woman's pelvic area, without touching her physical body but rather emitting vibes and receiving energy messages from the force field around the body. Teeteryngh would suddenly whirl like a mad dervish, pulling spirals of negative and repressive energy from the sex centre around the lower chakra in a huge snaking plume of invisible discharge, leaving the woman before him entering, totally submissively, ecstasy of the body. This ecstasy, crucially, was to be experienced as something which was in the body but not of the body; this release allowed the energy patient to sense that the body was simply the vessel through which life is lived. It was not them. People would be liberated and find that their body was theirs alright, a bit like their car might also be theirs, but it would have to go in the end. This was where the confrontational techniques came in handy. If a woman, for example, failed to let-go in a deep acceptance of her sexuality and mortality all at once, Teeteryngh might invite others in a group to gather around the subject for a hot-seat energy discharge. The client had to express their rage in response to negative feedback, the discharge of negative energy their fellow groupees chose to hurl at them, full face. Interestingly, though, whereas in Vamoosh's and Gavin's hot-seats people used words, in Teeteryngh's experiences people emitted funny noises instead, shaking and making faces.

The combination of the two techniques had so invigorated Niyati, especially since she thought that noises rather than words might help her accelerate the healing of her linguistic disability, that when she had heard that Teeteryngh would be coming to Khatahpult she had taken to doing dynamic meditation three times a day in preparation. Her best hope was to be invited to work as his assistant. That would be a little like being a magician's aide without the need to wear a tiara. Rather the meditating would, she hoped, through stripping her bare rather than dressing her up, support her quest to become the hollow bamboo Teeteryngh required his assistants to become. In large groups Teerteryngh could not always get to everybody, and the bamboo served to capture fall-out from him and transmit it to those he could not reach. Mindful of the negativity with which she had infected Gavin, Niyati worked very hard to get ready for the big man.

The London centre buzzed and so did Niyati, especially when invited to assist at Teeteryngh's debut performance for Khatahpult. On the night, two hundred freshly washed sannyassins paid £5 and climbed the stairs to the top of the warehouse, since the lift had been sterilised and reserved for Teeteryngh's use. The vast meditation space, across the entire floor of the warehouse, had been scrubbed three times from top to underlay by thirteen visiting German sannyassins who had recently learnt from Vamoosh that they were full of guilt and must find physical work meditations to help them let go. Violettah, the centre leader, in a special orange boa bought specially and a ring which glowed in the dark around the locket of her mala containing Bhagwan's face, led Teeteryngh to the podium and, as he raised his arms in the air, 200 people jumped, shouting WHOO. Then, from the new double woofer amplifier, some other-worldly Vangelis switched the mood of the room and Teeteryngh moved between dancers, tweaking and fine-tuning their screwed-up aural energies. As the music died away, the lights dimmed and Teeteryngh gently intoned,

"You are asleep. You are asleep," then suddenly boomed, "Wake up! Wake up!" A huge puff of theatrical smoke and a pop and a sizzle preceded a blast of the sannyassin shuffle from the new sound system and Teeteryngh disappeared. This was where Niyati had an active role. To the left of the podium there was a short stretch of curtain; behind this, a wheelchair. It was Niyati's job to guide Teeteryngh from the podium, behind the curtain and into the wheelchair. Then she was to hurry him, pushing smoothly yet rapidly, and descend with him to a waiting Alfa Romeo with air conditioning. It was essential that Niyati should not disrupt Teeteryngh's equilibrium during the transition from meditation space to vehicle and, in view of this, Niyati had got up extra early and done the dynamic meditation, twice. She hoped this had done the trick.

The next day, Niyati received her invitation. Violettah handed it to her as she moved towards the lift after morning dynamic meditation to have a cigarette with the sausage workers downstairs. Niyati had been requisitioned to act as personal assistant to Teeteryngh and support him while travelling, working, sleeping, eating, meditating and following his intuition in Brazil. It was, in effect, a secondment for Niyati from Khatahpult and, although it was to last just three weeks, it was considered one of the highest accolades any sannyassin could ever be afforded. Of course no one ever said so for fear of feeding an Ego.

1980

II

Teeteryngh wore orange pyjamas, a waistcoat and a woolly pointed hat to travel. On special occasions he wore a long orange robe, freshly pressed. Like all great men he was a sensitive type, and Niyati's job was to minister to his needs. He could only drink coffee from a particular bean. The coffee could not be ground in advance and would be embittered by unfiltered water. Filtering was not the norm in 1980 and the logistics of feeding him coffee on the long flight to Brazil meant that Niyati had to refer back to Physics and Chemistry O levels, circa 1972. His rooms had to be especially pristine, there being something unique about the Western mite absent from its Pune cousins. Music, especially, resonated within him and the quality of sound could alternately send him into ecstasy or a paralysis of agony. Women's energies, in particular, might affect him adversely. It was necessary for his body, however, the connection between his material and his spiritual body being only tenuously maintained, that he sleep with a woman every night. She was intuitively plucked, daily, from the infinite entourage of sannyassins drawn around him, when her energies balanced and attuned with his, thus earthing him. It was interesting to note that younger sannyassins, who had perhaps had less time to accumulate toxins in their auras, were generally chosen over older women.

Given the implications of Teeteryngh's particular set of contra-indications, Niyati wasn't expecting the journey to Brazil to be easy. She took very little luggage of her own as she prepared to lug his two allergy-resistant Yves St Laurent suitcases from pillar to post. She thought she was going to die when she spilt her (instant) coffee in his lap on the way across the Atlantic as she tried to brush a crumb from his eyebrow, but recovered. When she was frightened by the turbulence, Teeteryngh assured her that his presence on board would at least preserve them both from crashing.

Three orange people met them at Sao Paulo airport and they drove, high up in a van, past corrugated iron housing sprawled along the edges of the dual carriageway. Defecation. Polluted squalor. India-like with all the added bonuses concomitant with the technological advance of the West. In the countryside, a homogenised condominium in pristine white protected them from the horror of others' real lives while they got on with the business of changing the state of the world.

Teeteryngh's specialism was working silently with large groups. This meant that, generally, if the group stood in a circle and Teeteryngh was in the room, everyone would swoon and fall over. Some people, especially men, were of course resistant. Teeteryngh would have to approach them, rubbing his hands together and suddenly throwing his arms out towards them, targeting them with whooshing energy, spiralling swiftly with a magician's precision of aim, hissing and firing like a steam train, to work on them. Then they would go. Some, falling, would shake in waves of orgasmic pleasure. Others would lie ecstatic on the floor, eyes turning back in their heads like the Indian people during Hindi camp; still more, the Germanic types, would cry and scream and think they were in the cathartic stage of the dynamic meditation. These last had to be claimed.

By association, as Teeteryngh's assistant, Niyati had the same effect on the men as Teeteryngh had on the women, which quite surprised her. Once their deep let-gos subsided, and they could stand again, she was even more surprised to find that they all wanted to sleep with her. It was a bit like being one of Fleetwood Mac.

One, Kamal, at the end of the group, took her to a beach: a beautiful white sanded postcard with palms and crystal clear sea. His house, at the top of the cliff, was hers, he said, and Teeteryngh's, if they'd like to stay a week. But Teeteryngh caught a cold, which menaced that tenuous link between body and soul, and Niyati had to make an emergency exit, a witness to her negativity, to service his baggage needs.

Returning to the London meditation centre as an assistant to Teeteryngh radically altered Niyati's standing and, as life in a Hackney high-rise with fewer and fewer visits from Gavin started to drain from her the little energy she had left, she soon found herself dreaming of Pune. This time Niyati's one-way ticket to India was provided at Khatahpult's expense since she was to travel with a consignment of books for Bhagwan. Only one whose energy had been tested and verified by Teeteryngh might handle books for Bhagwan and in the event they had struggled to find anyone suitable but her. Niyati felt her surrender to life as a devotee grow easier as her connection to the master gained currency.

She planned to leave the West for life and envisaged that she would enter the ashram as a permanent resident and hopefully an 'energy medium' in her own right. Life as Gavin's partner was a dream she was trying to forget. Luckily she had managed almost completely to drop identification with her earlier life, and she very nearly forgot to tell her parents she was leaving in June.

Niyati phoned Gavin. It was the first time she'd felt in a strong enough position to do so, although he'd written and been to see her once or twice and before she'd been to Brazil. As the wind blows. She needed him to know.

"Gavin"

"Niyati. Hello my love. I was just thinking about you. How are you my sweet?" She could hear James Taylor playing in the background.

"I'm fine; really well. Really good. Yes. Thanks. What are you doing?"

"Well, now, there's a question. Your place or mine, baby?" His idea of a joke.

"Now you put it like that, you know, maybe I'll come and say goodbye?"

"Yeah, I heard. Pooners, eh? The old Bagwash got you again, dirty old bastard." Another joke.

"Yes. I'm going to Pune. Tomorrow. For ever."

"Now, that's a really, really, lauuuung time."

"Um. Well, you never know."

"So. Yeah. You're getting wise, are you? Growing up some? Getting your head round the fact that this place ain't big enough for all of us. Someone's gotta go, every day, huh?"

"Gavin. I know and you know, I have a lot of love for you and I was thinking of coming to see you?"

"Come now."

She hitched up the M1 and rang him from the services.

They walked past the Welcome Lodge, round the lake, to his bed and stayed there until she had to go. As she crept from the bed at dawn, he said,

"Niyati. Pune. Take care, my love," and turned his face to the wall.

1980–1981

Arriving in India, this time prepared and on her own, Niyati was armed against the assault. She had change ready for the porters, and the guarantee and receipt for the latest Sony double-cassette player were tucked into the back of her passport. She struggled through customs with racks of cassettes and a small bag of cotton clothing that would last until her next trip to Pune town.

She suffered a taxi drive all the way to Pune, stealing herself against fear as the car skidded too close to the edges of deep ravines, narrowly missing the hurtling painted lorries on every bend. She'd a room ready in a high-rise apartment, all of three floors, with a window onto an inner courtyard into which residents emptied buckets as if into a Hogarthian gutter. She slept for a day, easing slowly into the rhythm of her new life and waking in time for morning discourse on day two.

Seville Court had hardened its expression, tidying begging to the end of the road to make way for parking for rickshaws and no-entry signs. A hexagonal bookshop to the left of the gate sold tickets to fully paid-up members of the material world.

The porch at the back of Aum House, where discourse had once been held, could no longer accommodate the morning seekers, and a grand, round auditorium, Transformation Arena, had been erected in the space once borrowed for high days and feast days from the people next door. Five pairs of sniffers vetted them now so that any hint of deviance from flavourless anonymity might be nipped in the bud. Hindi camp was a thing of the past, Bhagwan catering daily for up to a thousand Westerners at his feet. Niyati listened to the plaintive far-off wail of the steam trains, shushing, and the strange crooning birds. She shared the floor with wave upon wave of seekers billowing outwards from the podium where now a microphone poised expectant over the raised chair. Krishnu stood behind the platform, waiting for Bhagwan's chauffeured car as it glided, silent-humming, along the drive from Aum House to deliver the master to devotion. Krishnu bent to open the door, bolting upright again, hands in namaste pose, his eyes darting wildly about the crowd, protecting his charge.

Bhagwan's grace, as ever but with a wider reach, beamed from the stage as he slowly turned, as if gently revolved on a dumb-waiter, by degrees, hands held together before him, sweeping the carousel-crowd with his love.

"And the first question: …"

Niyati rose, stiffly, after nearly two hours' spontaneous discourse from Bhagwan, to find her shoes from rack on top of rack, built into the roadside bank beside Transformation Arena. Nobody spoke as she wound her way through to main reception, the stark grey house now clad so brightly in seamless marble it almost disappeared from view into the morning brightness. Rows of women stood in for hard-nosed fat South African Venus who, promoted, ran an empire from the back office and, hearing Niyati had arrived, sent a small

French mouse to find her.

Bird-like Leela, Bhagwan's personal secretary since his first notoriety in Bombay in the early 70s, was no longer vetting seekers for darshan. Instead, Venus sent Niyati straight through to Arump, a large, shining Dutch woman who allotted her a priority slot for that evening's meeting with the master.

"Good, Niyati. You're here for good? No going back?"

"No going back. It's now-forever, Arump."

"Good. It was good with Teeteryngh, yes? Bhagwan has been waiting for you." Niyati took this the wrong way, forgetting the ego, and danced elated home for a shower, unwrapping a special darshan robe, only to be dejectedly ejected at the evening gates for smelling rather strongly of hamsters. Twice more the sniffers shunned her until, finally, five days later, she sat scrubbed raw at the feet of the master.

Bhagwan no longer spoke but five long, lithe and frenzied women danced at her back as the master gently touched her third eye, dissolving residual resistance to surrender. The energy was flowing. Twelve wild musicians beat drums, zooped guitars and played in a florid passion which flooded the jungle surrounding Bhagwan's extended back-porch and the sea of fiery seekers. He sent her back to her spot of the floor, leaning towards Arump to whisper the message, which came the next day. Bhagwan had selected her as a medium for his energy. She too would dance nightly for his grace.

By day she worked in the front office, scrutinising the newly arrived, putting them through their paces. Some she sent to work meditation, scraping new accommodation from the dust. Others joined her secret gang of darshan guards, who watched over their master more rigorously each day as, as with all who pose a threat to the established order, threats were made against his life. Secret meetings were held by strategists to decide where best to plant select and watchful seekers who sat in discourse and in darshan, with their backs to the master, perusing the crowd.

By night, as the music roared, she danced for Bhagwan, a hollow bamboo, transport for his energy to the too-many would-be realised human beings who flooded into the small hill-port. Three hundred then four, five hundred came in the evening; too many for individual meetings with the master. And in the morning, two and then three thousand sat at his feet.

Niyati moved from the high-rise apartment, to a hut which Premda, a permanent devotee now too who lurked in the undergrowth, had built before he'd moved on to lodge with a wealthy American model. This hut she shared with Sufi, the mother from Tushita, and young Saffron, while the children's father, Saturn, still suffered fatherhood with Scarlet at Tushita. Sufi and Niyati's hut had a veranda with bench seats looking out through trellis to the settlement built in the grounds of an imposing colonial residence. A makeshift shower, dead centre of the clearing, stood in for television. Behind the veranda, slatted dividing walls and a bed. To its side, a high-placed slab held the kerosene stove: sugar, tea, and the comforts of home, and sometimes a bandicoot, which was not nice. Above, an attic roof and monkeys toying with twine over Saffron as she slept.

One night a buck-handsome-Aussie machetéd his way through the woven walls to ravish her as she slept. Another night Premda called, rampant and steaming his way through both Sufi and Niyati: life, sex, non-possessive love the name of the game. Such dating practices branded the movement and were only occasionally arrested in honour of epidemic infestations. Periods of abstinence, enforced on medically meditative grounds, offered brief respite from saying 'no' to 'no' and 'yes' to 'yes'. Word came from the central office and spread fast-furious through the grapevine. Similarly, crazes grew. Several Tushitans, now dotted throughout the Indian commune, had elected to be sterilised. One young woman, Ghatoh, 23, lay in her flowery bower recovering from the general anaesthetic, easily procured during Indira Gandhi's push to limit the expansion of India's population. Ghatoh had returned from hospital, sterile.

"I just feel so blessed."

"Why?"

"Why, Ma? What a question. When I first opened my eyes, I felt in bliss. Liberated. Set free. Grateful to existence for this freedom. This freedom to follow my path. My divine journey."

"But," (a word Niyati seldom allowed herself) "you have changed the body to fit with an idea you have about a particular path. Are you sure you've done the right thing?" Ghatoh looked really weird. She was lying, puffed up like a whale with her pale skin pimpling, in the light of the moon shining through the leaves and the bamboo woven walls of her lofty hut.

"Now I am pregnant with myself," she explained, and Niyati had to admit that she did look a bit like she'd swallowed herself whole. "Now, I can devote my entire life to seeking without the interruption of motherhood." Niyati thought about Megan and Ben and Gavin's careful washing line.

"I'm not sure I agree with this."

"Well, can you leave now, then, Niyati?" asked Ghatoh. "I need to focus inwardly and your extreme negativity is giving me a headache."

1980–1981

II

Niyati, shunned by increasing numbers of sterile friends, was cheered when Gavin sent a letter, some sweet marmalade with a jibe about Tushita's bitter brew and some biscuits. Nice and Custard Creams. He didn't know about the special biscuit shop in the MG road. He also sent a letter, all capital letters interspersed with late night swirly paintings that said, 'I love you', although he didn't use the words. He wrote about the Elms, Dutch elm disease and a new back fence made from untreated wood. He wrote about the path along the lakeside that ran from his house to the motorway services and he told her about riding bareback through the Buckinghamshire seasons. Distance makes the heart seem stronger.

Starved out, sexual infection went into remission and the all clear was given. 'Just say yes', the Pune norm, resumed. Nightly, dubious suitors pursued her from darshan when, fatigued from conducting Bhagwan's energy, Niyati would reluctantly accompany one or the other to the Zorba bar, which served White Russian cocktails, Gin Lime Soda and

Kingfisher Beer. Ashram-run, with entrance only available to a Western clientele, and imitating a Caribbean beach-bar with reggae blasting from tree-hung speakers, the bar played host to chit-chat-free chat-up, which was tricky to say the least. Lines ranged from, 'Wow, feel the energy between us' to 'I just have a feeling to be with you tonight. I need to surrender to that'. It wasn't really feasible to turn another away unless they were pushing the river, rather than going with the flow, of course.

She'd visited an Ayurvedic doctor in town who'd smiled, knowingly, and laid her flat on his couch. Not speaking, but feeling her womb and her breasts, he'd poured thirty, small, dark, round pepper-corn like pills into a tiny paper packet. One to be taken nightly but not when the full moon shone and come and let me feel you again very soon. She had had to give up on Microgynon 30, finding it puffed her up, Ghatoh-like, in the middle of the month but this magic potion worked just as well. A mystery, or perhaps she was simply lucky. The body was only the body, after all.

A couple of sannyassin women she knew, opting to delay sterilisation for later, had visited a clinic in town to suck out their unborn children. Both suffered the agonies of the damned and pelvic infection, which rendered the sterilisation operation unnecessary. Others came with children already in tow and abandoned these to the school, where they learned anything or nothing as they chose. Saffron would jump from her rickshaw on her way in the morning and wander the side streets, sharing her lunch with those who took it from her. Scarlet had simply screamed and raged against the silence of surrender until they had sent her back to Tushita and the order of a village school. Niyati stuck to her small, brown Ayurvedic pills and kept her mouth shut as she tried to silence the ceaseless inward chatter of protestant ethics.

The stakes rose daily in tandem with the swelling numbers of faceless seekers. To escape the crowd, sannyassins like Niyati who had made the commitment to stay forever longed to be granted ashramite status, a rare accolade given to those who'd proved devotion and relinquished attachment to the material world. When the time came, Niyati moved to a small muddy hut at the side of Transformation Arena which she shared with a silent, solitary German seeker who refused with stoic resolve to engage in conversation and cup washing. Later, a transfer gave her a mattress in a room the size of two beds, which she shared with three others. Vivacious Niyati disappeared.

To maintain her service Niyati was given a number, a photo identikit label to swing from her mala and a pass for a tray of food, twice a day. Hot, strong men and women peered over boiling vats of water and oil while others sautéed strips of tofu, shaken with soy sauce. Once, a woman fell into a vat of oil and died and a crazed moving snake of celebrating orange people rushed her deserted body to the burning ghats where a queue had formed. Three others, the indigenous dead, had to be disposed of first as their mourners wailed and praised, and sneered at the Western initiates. Watching, as the sun sank and the pyre-flames of the oil-fried girl gave up the ghost, Niyati mourned.

Something was wrong with the ashram but Niyati couldn't work out what it was. There was a lot she couldn't discuss. As a resident, an ashramite, there was never any need for her to move beyond the ashram gates. Beyond, enclaves of sannyassins lived in huts amongst the trees, playing music, chattering and running imaginative import-export enterprises to keep them in pocket. Inside, Niyati moved slowly from her mosquito-netted corner to the dark recess behind the main office. Here she sifted through incoming mail: a special job. As she read seekers' letters to Bhagwan she could see herself as she had once been and as she touched the paper she could feel the pull of a drawer in her mother's room, stuffed with Basildon Bond. She passed these cries to one who chose Bhagwan's quotes that these might wake them up. As enquiries swelled it became Niyati's job, not Bhagwan's, to choose their names and send them in the post. Later still, when demand far outstripped supply, new sannyassins, disappointed, found they were lumbered with their original names. Rebirth changed its face.

Stepping from main reception's air-conditioning at midday, Niyati held secret meetings with the guards in a tin-lidded hut. Blood boiled and requests were made for arms. Niyati's mind chattered while she looked for answers but Bhagwan, even, had stopped talking. In the morning discourse, now, as five thousand sat at his feet, she sat amongst them, watching her guards watching him and watching herself watching herself. At night, now, darshan was a soup of dancers, the mediums' numbers swollen to melt in the sea of starving seekers.

Later still, more secret meetings for a select few re-commissioned ashramites, sending them daily and with slow discretion to the four corners of the globe. Bhagwan was leaving and she too must go away. America via London, spreading chosen words with care.

A friend arrived from Tushita and asked if Niyati would meet him in town. She found an hour and slipped into another world.

Outside the ashram gates, bitter business raged across the street. No more the benevolent leer of the man without the body, face big lipped. Now, in his place, the women with their damaged charges, worn by rage, tore her robe as she tried to pass and they had learned a few more words.

"You bad, greedy, europe-whore. Give me money. Give. You die." Beyond, the boy with the chai-stall held his own, plying new arrivals with a weakened brew in a row of tall glass tumblers, raking it in. The street had gained a permanent resident at its end, a curled corrugated iron sheet serving as a permanent shelter to a man who had lived in the ditch. Dark, shining, dried bullocks' dung smeared evenly across the ridged construction offered him insulation from the sharp tapping of passing peers who rapped on his roof with sticks and jeered at his social-climb.

Niyati climbed in a rickshaw, the meter ticking, a new surcharge already levied for the devout by a fresh-pressed driver with a sharp eye for business wearing jeans. He didn't smile but threw his head back with his question,

"Where?" sharp shot through his lips.

"Music House, please Baba."

"Music House. Music House. Pht." He hard twisted his throttle, kicking up dust to bully his way through the throng. Niyati paid and he asked for a tip. Intimidated, she dug deep, handing over what she could and he spat on his hand.

All around, in the bushes once thronging with hut-dwelling bright-faced sannyassins lay the signs of evacuation. The roof of Sufi's hut had bowed inwards, weighing the soft-woven front of the veranda and capsizing their warm home. In the clearing around the shower, creepers crawled up and around the makeshift tables with their upturned tinny barrel-stools, to form a barrier which blocked entry to three of the huts on the other side of the close. Two or three small groups of stoic seekers remained in the emptying village, well stocked with the looted paraphernalia one might need for luxury-hut-life. Niyati's friend, Sujan, emerged from a group of five brightly orange crusaders, his arms spread wide and open to catch her, crying.

They moved slowly together through the long paths that sannyassins had cut from the undergrowth as the sub-commune had first expanded and then contracted. They picked their way through the busy afternoon traffic of daily Pune life and found a dusty café with aluminium seating and round sticky tables to match. A boy delivered Thumbs Up in swirly bottles with straws. Children swarmed in and around, still asking her the time, tapping wrists. Sujan was not happy.

"What's going on, Niyati. Come on. I've just got here."

"I can't say."

"You know I've been saving for months, working in that bloody power-station, just to get here."

"That's so good, you know. That must be so good, Sujan. To stop now. To be."

"Well it's not is it? Now, here I am and everyone's leaving. You've got to tell me. What is going on?"

"Well, you know Sujan. There are rumours you know? But sannyassins, they're gossips, aren't they?"

"For fuck's sake, Niyati. Look, you know. I know you know. And, you look fucking awful."

"Thanks Swami. I accept your feedback. I'll watch that. How I feel, you know. Bhagwan says . . ."

"He doesn't, does he? He doesn't say fuck all anymore, does he? When I heard he'd stopped talking, I - he has, hasn't he?" Niyati nodded. "Yeah. Gordon Bennett. I just don't get it. What the fuck? What kind of brain-dead idiots does that make us? I don't get it, this one."

"You're, um. When you talk to me with such hostility, I feel, um."

"Look. I'm really depressed. That's the truth. I can't believe, well. Look. Can I stay with you tonight? Please. I'm asking because I like you, none of that right-on non-

136

possessiveness stuff. I'm no good at that. Nice idea but, well, can I?"

"Yes. As you put it so nicely." She smiled.

"And can I go to discourse, sound of one hand clapping bloody discourse, with you, tomorrow?"

"Yes, ok. Yes, you know, I'll be working, with, um. Yes, we can go to the ashram together, yeah and I'll find you tonight, when I finish. Around nine. Ok? Only, I've got to go now. We'll talk later. Ok?"

"Well, yes. That's good. I'll see you. I'll meet you back at the ashram, then. And we'll go to my place. It's a nice hut. Fantastic. All mod cons. Ha. It used to be Mondeo's." The irony was lost on Niyati as she flagged another rickshaw and watched the tattered and fraying clothing that the God she loved had wrapped around Pune, passing.

Niyati met Sujan and played house for the night. He had a stove of his own and a bed, high on a wooden platform in a room to himself. They talked but she held her secret as close to her chest as he kept her close to his. Hugging, warm, all night, no pressure, they parted friends at the ashram gates and waited in discourse. But Bhagwan never came.

Bhagwan left the commune just as she knew he would. She waited on the path with the few who knew his car would pass that way. She hoped he had known her as he passed and smiled.

1981

III

Niyati's sister was just leaving for work when she rang the bell. They'd worried a lot and Gavin had been phoning weekly but no one could tell where she was or what she would do next. Now here she was, wrapped in a shawl and carrying a small maroon holdall bearing a Qantas sticker, on the doorstep of a large W2 flat.

"Oooo, it's you. Super." Her sister beamed, throwing open the door in her petticoat, a mascara wand in the air. "I'm so relieved. I didn't know. I. . ." Niyati faltered and they went inside to the teapot and some toast.

She stayed for three weeks, on and off, wandering from room to room of a vast London flat, while her sister left and worked. Then she borrowed some makeup and a handbag to get a job that would start in a month.

She'd kept a prior engagement and crossed London to a small leafy retreat, which kept warm and safe Pune's upper-echelon evacuees. The ashram had sent her to continue her work in London to prove herself before a new life in the

American ashram, where Bhagwan would be. She had to report to Titania, the Mistress of the Full Moon. Titania looked her up and down and she crumpled.

The London streets were alien yet flavourless. The bus, full of those who looked away; a silent conductor and unacknowledged travellers who communicated only via a system of bells. Passers by, robotically moving on seamless tracks. Shops, loaded and flashing in neon Technicolor or subdued white, red and blue. Other rundown stalls, chipping paint and windows plastered in signs. Women and pushchairs; new hippies with babies slung in corduroy on their mothers' fronts; the elderly drunk in torn tormented tweed; shuffling homeless; litter blowing and sticking. Niyati closed down her gaze, frightened that she might intrude and they'd then get her. She clutched an *A-Z* yet hid it from those who might then know her innocence.

Niyati located Titania's lair and climbed into the lowered pit that gave the house its dank foundation, buried as it was beneath a layer of dripping undergrowth, turning upward to creep from the base to the roof.

Inside the coven Titania stood, central, in pale, slender, muted orange, sleekly fitting floor to ceiling. Her pale blue eyes stripped experience from Niyati who quaked like a five year old first at school. All around reposed bearded deep men supping lemon grass brews and spelling out strategy over a couple of maps and a *Sannyas* 1981 diary.

"Well, Niyati. Why should I find you work here in the commune?"

"Titania. I'm here in transit to America. Venus sent me."

"Venus. Venus. Venus. You'll have to drop that ego trip, Ma. Venus doesn't care. She will be waiting, waiting to see if you cling to this idea that you are closer to him, to Bhagwan, because you are a medium, or not."

"But, I, er, I was in the office there, and co-ordinator of the darshan guards and an ashramite and so I, um, I . . ."

"And so you made an assumption, Ma. And your assumptions are your issue and you will have to go out into the marketplace and prove to me, to the commune, that you are ready to drop this 'I'."

"Yes."

"So, Niyati. You come back and see me in eight weeks, yes?"

"Ok. Yes Titania."

Someone hairy, listening, came to rescue her and offered her a cup of tea.

"Raspberry, mint, lemon grass, mixed herbal infusion?"

"No thanks. I think I'll, er, I think I'll go." The man offering tea held out his arms and she fell into the folds of an orange, rough woven, quadruple knit, wrap-over jacket. He steered her up and out of the pit and onto the open road.
She'd paced the streets, fast thinking and stopped at a phone box to call her sister at work.

"Can I borrow some stuff? Clothes? Make-up? I think I'll go for that interview after all."

"Of course. I'm so glad."

In the course of a day Niyati travelled into the cellars of North London and shimmied up the higher floors of a comforting Promotional Agency in Covent Garden. After some reflection she accepted the job offered, to start as autumn began, as general office assistant, and imagined she'd be joining those she thought she could beat rather than those she knew she couldn't.

1981

II

Having secured an ordinary job, Niyati had a month in which to attend to affairs of the heart. And on the ninth ring,

"Yup."

"Gavin?"

"Yup."

"It's Niyati. I just got back from Pune."

"Oh, wow. I was so worried about you. I thought you were coming back, you know, your old lady, your sister, she thought. Where the fuck have you been? What happened to you, girl? You never heard of communication?"

"You, Gavin? You what? As far as I knew, I left to go there forever. So, where's all this coming from about, you know, coming back? Times? Dates? I never said I was coming because, well, I wasn't."

"Yeah. Well, you know, girl, I knew you couldn't have done that. Come on. You couldn't resist me. I knew you'd come back."

"I don't believe you. You haven't changed at all."

"You'd better believe it baby. So, when you coming to see me? Come on, girl. Just play it like it is."

"Ok. You're on. You're right. I can't wait to see you. So. Now? How about I get a coach in about, I don't know, about an hour?"

"That's my girl."

She left a note on the kitchen table for her sister, saying that she'd gone to see him. She took off the interview costume and slunk into a wrap around silk red dress with a pair of wedged espadrilles with laces that crept round her calves, running for the bus.

Gavin unravelled Niyati's lace-round-the-leg wedge espadrilles and threw them in the bin. He disentangled the wrap around silk dress and found her as he'd last seen her, inside.
"My Rosie" he said and it stayed.

She made a lot of jam and sandwiches, day after day, and they passed a month of summer looking at England again.

When she went back to London, in the autumn for the job, she sulked until he caught a bus to see her. He'd had a chat with a mate who'd sung him an Eagles song. Gavin felt he'd been out jumping fences for too long now. He knelt and asked, since he had found someone who loved him, if she would live with him before it was too late, but he warned her that she should not expect a commitment. Such an expectation would equate to imprisonment similar to the marriage which had killed his love for his wife.

Done deal. Rosie moved away from her sister in London to move in with Gavin who squeezed her clothes into an alcove at the top of the stairs. When the recession bit, she stopped travelling to work in London, doing freelance catering for local set-ups instead, as well as child-minding and stuffing envelopes for cash. Gavin travelled, running groups, healing the normally healthy neurotic world, while she visited a gestalt therapist regularly and for several years because Gavin explained she had projected the vast need that ran her life onto him rather than Bhagwan. He couldn't handle living with a leech.

1982–1993

To Gavin's chagrin, and quite against instructions, Rob was born in 1984, which upset the status quo. Bursting into the world, tidily between 9am and 5.33 on the first day of spring, Buddha-like, he showed her what love really was.

Gavin, trying hard, fitted new units, retiled the kitchen and installed a new gas cooker, which her mother bought. To christen it, he decided to scramble some eggs. There were two boxes on the side and he picked up the nearest.

"Will you use the others first? They're older," said Rosie. Gavin froze and counted to three. On the third stroke it will be not very nice.

He picked up first one and then the next box of eggs, crushing them into pulp in his right hand, before slamming his fists into the eye-level grill, which slumped over the four-ring hob.

"You fucking controlling fucking bitch. Get the fuck out." And she stayed.

He kicked a hole in the cupboard under the sink, head butted and remoulded the stainless steel draining board and then ripped a cupboard door from its brand new Moben case, scooping all the crockery into a heap on the floor. The two older children hovered beyond the back door until a neighbour took them in. Rosie, heavily pregnant with Freya, her second, raged against the monster:

"How dare you do this to our home. You crazy fucking prat," screaming and following him through the house to the top of the stairs where he kicked her away: falling, rolling, pregnant. Fearless, she gathered some clothes, raging as he went on, climbing, scratching past the monster to reach Rob, a two-year old, locked in with his Lego just beyond.

"Oh yeah. Fucking stir up a hornet's nest but don't stay to take fucking responsibility. You fucking arrogant middle class repressed piece of fucking shite. You fuck off to your fucking screwed up fucking family. Run home to mummy-darling but don't you fucking dare try and take Rob away from me." She'd grabbed the two-year old and strength that wasn't hers beat off the heavy walking boots, one resented ring, worn in lieu of a wedding to show he really did care, crunching into her face. His tirade spitted on. "You fuck off then you fucking dangerous piece of shit. The kids will learn you're a manipulative, dangerous fucking poisonous fucking cow. Fuck off. And don't come back."

She stayed away until the storm had passed and contrite and apologetic she returned, consolidating a habit. Freya, love itself, born in March 1987, eased the pain..

1982-1993

II

The Gestalt therapist was very good although she'd never worked with a sannyassin, ex or otherwise, before. In their first appointment she asked, "How do you feel Rosie?" and Rosie tore into a cushion, grabbing a truncheon which the therapist, who spent a lot of time on her own, kept for her protection by the door. Rosie thrashed the sofa cushions, roaring resentments about her mother who disallowed her anger.

"Good," said the vicar's wife who did Gestalt in her spare time. "Now, change places with the beaten cushion. The cushion represents, um, your mother. Am I right?"

"Yeah. My bloody mother."

"Ok, Rosie. Now. Relax. Breathe. Now move and sit on the cushion that represents your mother. Good. Now. Centre yourself. Think yourself into your mother's position. You can do this because we are all the many aspects of others that we have internalised. Right. Good. Now. What might your mother say? I'm going to repeat what you have just said to her and you find your mother's response. Ok? Right: 'Mummy. You're a complete fucking waste of space and you have never allowed me to express my feelings. You fucking cunt.' What do you say, Mummy?"

"Oh dear. Dahr-ling. I'm so sorry. I was only trying to do my best." Before the therapist could instruct her, Rosie fled to the other cushion, the one representing her, and bellowed,

"Trying? Fucking trying? Why don't you just fucking stop fucking trying and let yourself be?"

"And why don't you take your own advice, Rosie?" asked the therapist. "By the way, what have you done to your arm?"

"Oh. Gavin. He had a bit of a pink fit, yesterday, and hit it with a chair. He didn't mean to. He was trying to bash it into the table. To let out his rage, you know? My fault. I don't know when to stop. When to get out of his way. I need to learn to accept his feedback about me. I'm just very resistant. Lost the knack of surrendering when I returned from India, I think."

"And what might your mother say to that?" asked the very astute vicar's wife.

"My mother? What's she got to do with it?"

"Exactly. That's about time now I think, don't you? £15 today. Thank you."

The Gestalt therapist let her hints fall, especially when Rosie lost her three front teeth, putting the therapist in a very difficult ethical position, considering her loyalty to her peers, and Gavin's reputation in the field, but Rosie let her ramble on until she could take no more. One night in bed, just after she'd been away with the two youngest children, hers, sunning and swimming in a quiet corner of Europe, she turned away from him. Bright and early, threatening thunder, his birthday approached and she planned a party, to justify their recent marriage, to make him feel loved.

The house thronged with friend and foe, sickly sweet sponges and olives in a bowl. Gavin suffered the ordeal and his previous wife busied herself with cups of tea to relieve the faux pas he suffered under his new wife's naïve generosity of spirit. As Rosie swept French-bread crumbs into the bin, he paced the garden path and as she pushed the last chair under the new, replacement, veneer table Mark Weatherby had brought, he asked,

"Are you done?"

"Just about. Yes. It's not too bad, is it? Given we had so many here. So many different people. Wasn't it nice?"

"Nice? What the? Fuck me. How you could think. . . You don't know me at all. My worst fucking nightmare. All the fucking neighbours. Here. That's not a fucking birthdee. You? What? What the fuck are you on?"

"I'm sorry. I thought, you know. I thought, well. Cathy next door, and Jack, Sophia. They all help us out so much. They've been good to us, to me, to, since, well, as long as I've known them."

"Yeah. And it's not your fucking birthdee, is it? It's mines. And why the fuck would I want to be spending my birthday being grateful to the fucking neighbours? You tell me that."

"It's not your twentyfuckingfirst."

"Hostile fucking crap. You have not wanted to be with me, me, who I am. Not since your fucking holidee. Have you? You haven't fucking have you?"

"Where d'you get that from?"

"Last week. In bed. You're turning away all the time.

148

Make me feel like some fucking leper. You got a lot of fucking hidden agendas, girl. Don't you go laying all this at my fucking doorstep. Fucking partee. Hang it on the fucking wall," and he went out with the dog.

Days passed and they spoke a little. They tried to be polite and Rosie organised some recompense, a night in a wine bar. The sort of thing that couples do.

"I'm not fucking wearing a fucking dress shirt for this do."

"No, Gavin. Of course not. Your birthday treat. You come as yourself. I'm just wearing this dress because, you know, I don't get a chance, much."

"Good to see you outta corduroy for a change. Your arse looks fucking ace in that, doll."

"You don't look so bad yourself," said Rosie, thinking, but not being brave enough to add, 'You sicken me'.

"What time are we booked in to this do?"

"Well, it's not a do. Just turn up. I phoned and checked and they said there wouldn't be a problem." But of course there was.

Driving there, she was excited as well. A night out, being on show, with him. She remembered the buzz she had had when they'd first met. The anxious uncertainty of being with him, everyone suffering envy in the wings. She parked and they walked hand in hand to a bouncer who told them the place was full.

She shook and he sulked, criticising the food in a Chinese restaurant and complaining, afterwards, about the low fucking beams in an olde worlde pub. Tersely she said she was sorry but she could have done no more and she could maybe book for next week, turn up a little in advance.

"Car," he said, "I've had enough of this shite."

The argument which came next was her fault really. She

was a provocative cow but she couldn't take any more. As she turned the car and drove them away from the small town he snarled,

"Thank you for driving carefully through our shitty fucking pretentious fucking middle-class fucking wannabe shit hole." She snapped.

"Why do you have to go on and fucking on? Ok. So I fucked up your birthday. Big deal. I had the neighbours in. Oh, what a pain. The great Gavin Machim, being forced to discuss the merits and demerits of cheese footballs versus Ritz with a bit of cheddar. How fucking could I, eh? How could I do that to you? You spoilt fucking twat."

"Watch it. Shut the fuck up. Now."

"Oh dear. And then the big night out. Arrr. Wouldn't let you in to the wine bar. Get a fucking grip, you poor sad old fucking twat. When are you going to join the real fucking world? And the bloody money? Where do you think that came from for your inadequate, not fucking good enough fucking recompense fucking Chinese take away? Heaven? No. Fucking child minding, that's where. Looking after other people's children so you can fuck about in the garden, go fucking fishing. Do what the fuck."

"You fucking arrogant, fucking, hostile, fucking shitty controlling hostile fucking power fucking hungry bitch. Stop the fucking car."

"No. No I won't. You'll just have to get a taste of your own medicine for once, you self-obsessed fucking self-centred fucking ... No! ... No!" He grabbed the steering wheel and rammed on the handbrake, and they spun across the dual carriageway at 70 miles an hour while oncoming traffic startled to a skid, the car spinning, spinning to slide half into and half out of the ditch. She screamed and he threw her handbag, between him and the door, in the bushes before casting himself lose to run across the fields. The lights of oncoming traffic flashed towards her and she shook.

Still pale, she climbed out to get her bag and in again to find four wheels still had purchase enough to reverse and to turn. Fifteen minutes, shaking. Another ten, turning. She drove to a garage and went in, stunned, white, shaking.

"I've just had an accident. Can you?"

"Yes love. Petrol? Pump?"

"No, I. . ." The man behind the counter gave his friend, chatting silenced, a knowing look. "No. I - I just thought. It's ok. Sorry. I don't know what I'm doing. I - I'll just go." And she drove slowly through the night; life ebbed as she went with the flow.

Rosie crept into the house, after her error over the second birthday treat and he still wasn't there. Megan, babysitting for her younger siblings, started.

"You're early. You look - are you ok?"

"Yes, Love. No. I'm ok. Gavin's just gone to the garage. Fags, you know. Kids alright?"

"Well, you know Freya."

"I'll check," and she crawled in with her five-year old, who flung her arms round her neck and slept smiling and spitting on her cheeks.

Up early, hiding to school and back. Visit a friend. Don't mention the war but she plotted and struck when they were due out to dinner, a week or so later.

"Gavin. I. . . I can't do this anymore."

"Fucking dinner fucking parties. Tell me about it."

"No. I can't do this with you. I want us to split."

"Easy. The old Moslem way. I divorce thee, I divorce thee, I divorce thee. There you go. Happy now?"

"I'm not joking, Gavin. I need to end this, now."

"I've never been more fucking serious in my life, girl.

151

But you're not having the kids."

A bitter battle ensued since she could no longer think for herself and his friends had to do it for her, pointing out the errors in her logic. It's said it takes seven attempts before the abused can set themselves free and even at the eleventh hour, she was having second thoughts. He'd been warm toasty nice, the side she loved, and lay cuddled with Ben on the sofa. She dozed.

"Why am I leaving?"

"Search me," said Gavin. "You seem to have everything going for you here, girl."

She promised to try separation, a different bed, to see how things went, while continuing to see her counsellor and dealing with her inability to love. Properly. Until, in the dead of a winter's night when the weather bleakened, she gathered two children, her own, her mother's photograph albums and some toys, and fled, knowing somewhere locked away that it needed to be brought to a close.

1993–2003

We stayed with a woman on the Refuge's list, Gillian, until we could rent on our own. Freya, Rob and I squeezed in beside her two displaced boys in a council house made for three. Gillian, with a job, took the piss and I helped her with her nine to five; shopping when collecting her boys from school; polishing and preparing a meal. Mimicking a petulant partner, home from work, Gillian would throw her briefcase behind the door, her coat on the floor and shout, at 6pm, "Dinner, woman!" helping me move on. She helped with the social security, knowing her way round the game, and decorated once I'd found a home, two schools and some friends to share life.

My mother's photographs were given a wall in our new single home as I resumed identification with the past, trying to come to terms with the love I felt for colonials who had spent their lives issuing orders to an army of what they called, 'the Chinese'. There but for the grace of God go I, as my mother would say, visiting daily, having moved closer once Dad died, to make up for missed time, buoying us along.

Carefully established quite near a very new town, with all the accessories of normal life, like swimming clubs, an OU degree course to keep me off the streets, dinner parties and hangovers to suffer at work, existence adopted an even tone, the greatest excitement a curry, eaten sitting on the floor. I worked for a group of local artists, imported to give the new town grace, doing admin and arranging events, like groups without the abuse.

Within six years, spent working and trying to fit in, cleaning, cooking and struggling to establish firm rules, the kids stopped going to bed before I did. I found myself in a commune again, metamorphosing into my mother, asking for the volume to be turned down and our two-bed terrace, where the sofa was my bed and I shared a wardrobe with Rob, proved pressure-cooker tiny and we had to make a move.

We moved, on the wettest day of the year late in 1999, to a rented house in the middle of a field, just on the edge of the New Town's village, a bike ride from the schools. Rob had a room of his own with fitted carpet, a dartboard and an industrial surplus, under the bed, of muddy socks, crisp packets and coursework. There could have been anything in there; I didn't have my eye on the ball. Freya had a wardrobe big enough for all the clothes she wished she had and not quite enough to do at school. I had a fridge full of wine.

Nomadic, rootless in rented houses, I felt disconnected from the world I tried to join, and I craved and mourned the existence of another world. Here, in nature, in the cavernous house in the field, which had frozen us through four harsh winters, spring came with a vengeance in 2003 with trees, invisible before, bursting into existence and a rush of possibility on the wind. New leaves unfurled and optimism returned as if the seasons might not repeat again, tidily, one after the other with the idea that, perhaps, we might arrest time and hold off winter if everyone believed. Yet as the brand new millennium got underway, my optimism was tainted with a baleful unease and a desire for some of what I'd known before. I tried to tell Freya.

"You know, like people with Tourette's, they shout stuff out by mistake?"

"Yep."

"Well, I kind of talk to myself. I have conversations in my head about the way things are. You know? Work, education, cars, politics, supermarkets, and then, when I get to the part in the conversation in my head, I shout out loud the bad words like 'piss-take' or whatever."

"Well, to be honest, Mum, you might as well talk to yourself because nobody's listening."

"That's a bit harsh."

"Yeah. Sorry. I didn't mean that. You talk away. I like it really. Talk as much as you like. It's soothing, like having a radio on."

Haunted by my own propensity for wandering, inadvertently into disastrous situations as much as by my hunger for something beyond the everyday, looking back for a guide I captured an image of my mother, beside herself with her incomprehension of my teenage ingratitude, trotting out her best reproach:

"You know, as soon as you are out of the way, I shall be free to pick up whatever it was I put down once you came along. Only *this time,*" and here she'd pause to emphasise her stress and so repeat, "*this time* I'll have the benefit of hindsight." This 'hindsight' too was given particular attention by her glance since this was something no one could ever have unless they'd got to 'her age'. I persuaded myself that hindsight did away with the need for thought before action since I had moved on and away. Perhaps I'd find an ordinary kind of love to while away the years, one that would not be too demanding. I thought an affair might do, with someone I would meet on a train or in a pub. We'd arrange clandestine meetings on day-after birthdays and I'd have dates with a man who'd be pleased. Refuge Gillian's friend, and my friend, Sarah, had an idea, sweating up and down on her aerobic step beside me in the old church hall. The internet might provide the key.

miserablemates.com was a new website through which your friends could advertise you to others. The advantage of this method, for users on both sides, was the sense that no one had been desperate or foolish enough to seek love on the net. We were all there, quite simply, as victims of others playing cupid.

My profile, submitted by Sarah, for vicarious pleasure (since Sarah's husband Dave's name had lost its prefix 'shaggable' when he turned 50 in 2001) read like this:

"1956, UK made; masses of hair and baggage but space for more; 56,000 miles on the dial but has probably been clocked; keen to accelerate but fitted with calibrated brakes for responsive rather than reactive self-protection; easy on the eye with bohemian appeal; converted to alcohol-free fuelling; would fail emissions tests for smoking; rational expectations in view of age, gsoh, would like to meet sane man for refuelling."

I approached it like an armchair athlete watching Wimbledon on TV. A nice man, 'Old Timer' invited me for coffee, and 'Giveusago' sent some abuse, but the men in my sights, 'Hunky Harvey' and 'The BFG – Big Friendly Guy' were 'off the scene at present. Sorry and good luck'.

2003

As the summer of 2003 drew on, after the flurry of excitement when Premda had arrived and we'd had the reunion in the spring, my sense of restlessness increased. I grew disillusioned with the responses I was receiving from miserablemates for the desperately middle-aged. The computer told me 'you've got mail' but it was all junk. I remembered something from somewhere about active-participation. I decided to do the choosing myself. I didn't like beards and I'd had enough of being poor but something drew me to an interesting man in Wales. I didn't like Welshmen either but I reasoned that I might just stumble across the unexpected. I sent Welsh, bearded, Tom a message:

> I'm new at all this. Are you?
> How's it work?
> Enjoy the weekend.
> Rosie.

I was surprised to receive his reply. He was off to a gig, Vince Ray and the Razorbacks; he was a camper van driver who knew how trains worked and he had fought his way up in the music industry, while able to claim benefits for single parents.

I scoured the web and found an obscure Islington venue that hosted punk bands like Vince Ray and his crew, and found I knew nothing at all about those.

I had two sets of criteria: things I liked and things I felt I should really shy away from. Unfortunately, the best and the worst of my criteria both attracted top scores.

Attractive	5
Good	4
Mediocre	3
Dodgy	4
Bad-News	5

Tom's revelations gained full marks. He was very bright (very attractive: 5); he was flamboyant and creative, visually, musically and lyrically (very attractive: 5 but also very bad news compared with someone in accounting, another 5 so a 10). He was doing well in the music world, being more technical than creative (5 and 5) and he had responsibilities as a single parent combined with itchy feet (another 10). Even his friend's recommendation carried a veiled warning; he was complex like the rest of us. Very attractive and extremely bad news.

Tom wrote again, when he returned from the Smoke and provoked covert competition. We were pretty much level-pegging when it came to current lifestyles: not quite enough money; falsely modest about our careers, his in music – mine in the art world; a couple of grown-up-kids each but he issued a covert challenge, threw a gauntlet. Had we both had a legendary weekend? On Saturday, at Sarah's husband's party, I had suffered out of duty, feeling obliged to talk to the neighbours when Dave, the once shaggable husband and the star of the 52nd birthday, had vanished from his own do. I had ended the night clock-watching in Sarah's freezing summerhouse, kindly made available to smokers, while Dave's brother, Fat Graham, plying me with Chardonnay, tried to persuade me that Country Music, namely Dolly Parton, deserved a second chance.

"We're doing a gig. Come along", coaxed Graham. "You'll wish you'd heard us before. I'll keep an eye out for you; we'll have a drink. You'll see." Sarah, mopping up Chardonnay, nudged my knee, and whispered as I bent towards her to retrieve a lipstick from the floor,

"Rosie, I think you've pulled."

Knowing that real men were more reliable than cyber constructions, yet not quite ready to choose, I played a duplicitous game, agreeing to see if country could fill a gap in the real world as Tom warmed up on the side.

Hi Tom.

Yes! It was incredible.

I'm getting into the local music scene: it's not quite Vince Ray and The Razorbacks, more acoustic with guitars than punky-change-the-world but it makes up for the 9-5.

How was yours?

Rosie

Tom's night, trying to share a bed with his enormous(ly good) friend Julian, became only rock n' roll and I liked it. He was in-between the renovation and sale of a home he hoped to replace with a new life, since his business as a sound engineer was taking off. He wanted to know a bit more, what I did and about the kids, so I explained I worked as an arts administrator, somewhat augmenting my role while carefully playing it down, and that my kids were top of the list. I owned up to sannyas, perhaps he'd heard of 'the orange people', adding seasoning rather than spice, and with an eye to my advertised zest for adventure, I encouraged him in his dreams.

Hi Tom

I'd choose the motor home over the bungalow with a van, if you really want to take to the road for good, and £35 with that number of zeros seems a comforting amount so I'm assuming you'll get decent plumbing. So, wherever you are, you'll be ok and if you're short of money you can charge a fortune at festivals; if the sound business dries up, or the bands go off the boil, you can charge to use the loo.

And my other piece of advice is always follow that given by total strangers, who could be wewantyourdosh.com in Calcutta posing as a middle-aged woman from somewhere respectably tame, while seducing you into parting with your mortgage. Or not.

What next?

R.

He wrote, 'whatever happens, let's keep writing' and we did. We worked through status boxes, one by one; the website, miserablemates, had a 'mis-click' button, which took you to an empty page, like a phone box or a private room where you could leave a mis-click-story. Or you could mis-click-chat but that wasn't so popular. It seemed been-round-the-trackers like to keep their distance while they do their research. Or perhaps even that was too optimistic: who's going to tell the truth if they've screwed up their lives so much they have to resort to internet groping? We'd shared details of names and places and relationships, in part, but when I complained about an argument with my son who, at 19, still knew how to press all my buttons, I had imagined he'd write, 'kids, eh?' and tell me about his plans to tour but in the campervan, supporting Europe's stars. But instead he told me about his childhood and his guilt, letting me into my own life from the other side, writing, 'There's nothing like that love you feel for your mother, as a son but it's a horrible kind of love and I think they can be quite unpleasant, nasty, dismissive of their mothers, sons. I don't mean that I would be now, with my mother, but when you're about 19/21 even, about Rob's age and my son's age, it's that horribly embarrassing sort of feeling that you almost wish you didn't feel. It's stifling and you just know you've got to get away and that it's going to be a tear.' A tear, a wrench even and a hollow drone in the echoing home, a tree resists autumn. Rob and I were caught on the threshold feeling a sickness, a nausea Tom had felt and had no words for either, writing, 'your stomach sort of fills with this, I don't know, it's just embarrassing. I can't describe it. My Dad was no use so I was doubly burdened.' Tom unfurled his roots.

There was one of those days when you feel you've made a really dreadful mistake and after that there's nothing you can do except live with the consequences. I thought I had to stay with my mother for ever because I'd stopped her leaving. She had woken me up. We were all asleep, except for her, my mother. My Dad was asleep in the chair by the range which was going out and my mother came up and shook me in the bed. She said that she had to go but that in the morning I had to get my three brothers and walk with them to the bus stop and she'd meet us there. Anyway, to cut a long story short, I said that she couldn't go and leave us and that she had to stay and I remember her face and her sitting there on the top stair with her coat on. She didn't go and in the morning I thought she had made a terrible mistake. Well, I had really. I should have told her to go and then taken my brothers. I felt such a coward. I was 11 and should have known better.

I pictured Tom's mother's past in my own; small children and distress. Before Freya was born and after Rob. It was a day after a night before. The shattered pine table, stage centre; Rob's toys in a basket toppling into an upturned dog's bed, stage right; windows open back and front of a long thin, nicotine-stained room; dust in the light. Fearfully but with a stubborn sense of my rights, yet shaking, I filled a kettle and the back door flew open and flapped against the wall. "Out!" Gavin was big on imperatives.

I climbed upstairs, Rob still on my hip, and waited. The noise, as if clearing were being done in a wood-floored pub after a brawl, continued inside with an intermittent sound breaking through the bathroom window of the white, dry, clack of splintered pine planks falling to a growing pile on the concrete outside. Later, when the tidying stopped, muffled phone calls and the angry boil of the kettle.

Mark Weatherby came, ever faithful to his trainer. I saw him from my stair with Rob. He left the front door open, peering round towards the end of the front room and to Gavin,

"Gav. Let's. You gonna give me a hand with this, mate?" I sat on the third stair and bent to look. Mark, glancing a, "Hi, Rosie. Rob Rob," with a smile and Gavin threw me a shamed scowl. I let them put the table up. I said,

"Oh."

"It's oval. Fits in quite nicely," thought Mark.

"I don't think it's right." I was braver with Mark there.

"Well, don't look a gift horse. You."

"No. I mean. It can't be right that he smashes the table up and you bring this." Gavin shot out of the back door as Mark, dumb-fluxed for once, sat on a three legged chair and fell. "You not bringing us any fucking chairs then?" and I cried. Such cries.

It wasn't a terrific rebellion but it was enough to turn the tables. Gavin, distraught, toughed out his disappointment with himself and a softer man returned. There was a temporary reprieve; a comeback. It was probably September at the time.

Life went on. My feet hurt but I was happy; it was cold and the buttons across the front of my thick felt coat wouldn't button up. December and unknown Freya, buoying me along, would arrive in March '87. We were looking at door-fronts for kitchens and tempted by fantastical decorations in lime green and silver, to curse a Christmas or two, before falling onto the back seat of the bus on the way home; ferreting about in the dark. The bus driver occasionally coughing and putting his lights on. Giggling from the back, the single thread that tied Gavin to a sense of worth gradually fraying against the strain of a cursed inheritance, we lived on love again. But not long now. And each time, like Tom's mum, I'd get stuck on the stairs. Late January perhaps, time reassembles memory, Gavin proudly unveiled the new kitchen and moved towards the eggs.

Tom closed:

> Rob probably feels a bit guilty that you stayed there. It's terrible being a son. I read somewhere that you sannyassins were not going to have children. All about sterilisation. What happened to you then? There can't be a parent across the land who hasn't thought it might've been a good idea, at times, to remain meditatively self-sufficient. I know I do.
>
> Write soon.
>
> X T
>
> p.s. Is that your real name? Like my picture? I like yours – you changed it yesterday.

Hi Tom.

We left when Rob was 8. I don't think it's that although you never get rid of your ghosts, of course. I've been a bit of a nightmare; perhaps that's more like it. I screwed up. I can see how Rob would empathise with you over that push me pull you stuff but I can feel the same push me pull you with my own mother; and I so empathise with yours. Don't feel guilty; even if you had done as she asked, she might well have gone back again. Done it all again. Maybe.

It is my real name and I'm glad you spotted the new picture. It's a year or so old. Taken at the local music festival. Just quietly, not a fan of beards. You look a bit like the lead singer of Jethro Tull. Sannyassins weren't supposed to have kids but I wasn't prepared to surrender that much. Thank god.

It took me until I found myself in my mother's position to understand her. Something gaping in the impotence of having children who don't need you anymore; every cell still fighting for their survival; happiness; wanting to help; an emptiness I can't describe, a bile even, like the one you feel, the departing son, on the other side.
R.X

Four-year old Freya had had a post-office set which she played with for hours, filing and stamping and writing cheques. We had to bend down and put our noses six inches above the waft of dog hair, drifting across the pine floor, to establish whether our business was airmail or inland, TV licence, stamps, or just something for the scales, through the tiny perspex window she had at right angles to her legs, the shop counter itself open sitting flat on Freya's legs straight out, flat, carefully balanced.

Nothing crossed her while she concentrated on her sorting and her sums. But chaos disturbed her and even when the apparatus swung out from the walls of her new school to make a gym, she couldn't stand the change. The teachers would keep her somewhere else until they'd completed the transformation. She had seen too much too soon. If I went out, she had rituals to pass the time and lists and places for things to be while I left her with her family and she would confide her plans and strategies to me as if she had cracked a code that I had not quite been able to break. I think she shamed me into leaving in the end.

And if Freya had systems and things that could be kept in order in a case to guide her, I had to find a context for that. I realised that I knew almost nothing of the world outside. As Tom now sent cinematic scripts of a Britain I had left behind, a setting and context through which to articulate the defining moments of his life, he also drew a picture of a man. Not meanly do-able, like the run-of-the-mills looking for lonely divorcees in my near-by small town; not the powdery white of ecstatic emptiness, like Gavin, but an architectural construction, made of bones, sinew, pain and joy. He told me about his younger brother Stewart, his best ally in Northampton and a punk. Stewart had, to his envy, 'really looked the part' but if you visited their home, a council house in Northampton, there was something else going on entirely. He and Stewart had lived with their dad and two brothers, in a time when no one ever asked why their mother had a black eye and Tom willed the scene to life:

We'd all be sitting in a line anytime anyone came round, four brothers and our dad – him by the range in the comfy chair and the four of us all on straight back chairs and smoking. The place was a fog and you could hardly see through it. Really, there were these four paler spaces in the yellow of the wall behind our chairs that you could see if we stood up, from where our heads rested on the wall, protecting it as we smoked. Stewart, a convert from National Front to Punk, working in the Crown foundry, knew everything and when things were happening and where to be when. He was always up on the current events.

If you remember, you were probably still at school when it began, I was only 17 or 18 at a pinch, and then later there were the National Front rallies going on, once Thatcher was in, and demos against them in turn. Stewart had originally been in the NF and it was at one of these early rallies that he'd been stuck one side of the rioting, with the Police struggling to let him have his say, riot gear, the lot and he kind of saw the light if you see what I mean and the next week, funny really if you think about it now, the next week he was a punk.

I didn't remember. From then on, Stewart had galvanised action and Tom got carried along on the wave of activism via punk. Even when he'd left home, he relied on Stewart for the news. Stewart had had to leave Northampton, mid seventies; he'd upset a lot of people. But he'd got a council house by a racing circuit so it was alright in the end; he was a Grand Prix fan these days and a mechanic. He, Tom as well as Stewart, was edgy and cared about people who suffer and he'd fought to bring inequalities to the news. I was growing anxious, feeling inadequate in view of his politicism and I'd not had a partner with a conscience since Mondeo. But then he wrote:

Before, either you were a greaser or a skinhead and then you knew exactly who to fight, or in my case avoid, on your way home on a Saturday night. I never really seemed to be able to feel part of anybody's side and the main thing was that until I got a job I just couldn't afford the look. I was marked out for A levels – got them against the odds. What I really wanted was the proper two-tone trousers the skinheads wore but then again, by the time I had a job and a bit of money in my pocket, I didn't want to be identified as one of the skinheads. The skinheads started fights gratuitously but punks took action, positive action and I really quite approved of what they were doing. Anyway, as far as punks went, although I had some money it was a cheaper wardrobe than the one I would have had to have, had I stayed a skinhead!

As Tom put events in order, I thought of Freya, ordering things; and Bhagwan making us all the same. While my friends told everyone to call them something Indian with a meaning and throw away their Levis, Tom had had to knock himself about a bit, all to fit in. And, as Tom explained, because punks wanted to draw people's attention to the fact that life was painful, he had to steel himself against his own pain and stab himself through the cheek with a safety pin. I had simply had to dredge up phantoms to compensate for idyllic days in the benevolent English countryside with a patient father teaching me to love horses and appreciate agriculture. As Tom said, life was an uphill struggle for most people.

Ghostly reminiscences flittered in and out as I read Tom's story. In the quiet of the cavernous house where Rob's room was occupied increasingly by his absence, and Freya slept or read, studying her future, a door swinging lightly on its hinge beside me clicked back to close and served to remind me I had a new life and that Tom's application was still in progress. The dilemma was now to do with baggage and the fine line between honest disclosure and the advertisement of shoddy goods; yet I was drawn to the idea of a man who was willing to tell me so much. He kept hoping for a shared memory, it seemed, but if it was there, it was slow to emerge. Music divided us: although I knew the Clash I wasn't a fan but I appreciated the sentiment. James Taylor was alright but he thought all the songs were the same. And anyway, American stuff bothered him. He liked Punk. We advanced to mis:click:chat

TOM: There was one band you might remember. 'The Vibrators'. Remember?

ROSIE: No.

TOM: Their first album, god it makes me cringe, was called 'Batteries not included' and one of my mate's sisters was in it.

ROSIE: Sorry. Still no.

TOM: So we all went out to see them one night, this was once I'd got to Wales, which was pretty terrifying because the punk women were a new kind of woman really and I'd only had experience of my mother, as women go day to day in the past and what with the fashion sense and lack of money I'd not got close to many girls my age.

ROSIE: Is that what you tell all the women?

TOM: Well, alright. There was one, when school was coming to an end and she didn't care what I wore but that's another story. Anyway, I asked one of these scary women, one of 'The Vibrators', if she wanted a drink and she was so insulted and affronted, she kneed me in the bollocks.

ROSIE: Very punk.

TOM: I was lucky she didn't safety pin them to my wallet I reckon now.

ROSIE: Guess so.

TOM: It has to be said. I overcame my fear. Married her in the end. Slash (that's her name) so I suppose that's not very right on really although I lost her of course finally when the heroin became more attractive to her than I was. She ran away and left me. I had a two year old daughter and a tiny baby, my son, to bring up on my own.

ROSIE: When?

TOM: 1982. He's 21. She's 23 of course. But it saved my life, looking after the kids.

One to Premda; different aisles, same supermarket

Tom described the tear of leaving home at 18; the sense of deserting the family and going all the way to Wales, for a washing up job and the relief, having gone to escape his dad coming home from the pub or prison. He said the family were always in the papers so he was local news but terribly shy. Such mundane detail seemed to fill in for adrenaline. I decided to move things on.

Hi Tom.
I'll be in Glastonbury for a few days from Saturday and I was hoping we might meet? Are you free? XR

Hi Rosie, yes.
I can definitely make it to Glastonbury but only on Tuesday. Could we meet at 2pm? T. X

I confirmed:

Brilliant. I can't wait. Meet me outside the Assembly Rooms, on the high street, at 2pm. I'll be wearing a red and white dress and a million jumpers if it's cold. XX R XX

2003

II

I drove through the benevolent Sunday sunshine and beyond the nasty afternoon shoppers along leafy lanes and twisted turns to Glastonbury. The minute you pass the sign announcing the ancient spot, lettering changes from standard issue 'B & Q' to ye olde worlde scripte advertising: stones, carved; auras, healed; juice, organic. I had decided to visit Jan who had gone to tell her daughter about the idea of conversion to a life free of possessions of abstract and concrete varieties. Her daughter's house on the hill would serve as a perfect home from home after emigrating to free-love and ecstatic dance in a commune of retrogrades somewhere near Byron Bay, South West Australia. She and Premda intended to continue conversations about her plans which she had really only hatched at the get together when he'd first arrived in the spring. Now, in August, living with total freedom amongst people who still believed in spreading seed at random in order to reap a greater love-harvest was clearly going to be quite exhausting, and so she'd come to visit her daughter's house to make sure it would be a sympathetic residence and a retreat from Australia if ever she needed a rest. Now Jan was holidaying in a town which held with some of the ideals of 1976.

We hugged and I put my lap-top with my make-up bag on an airbed swathed in tie-dye. We ate home-roast and a salad and walked to a bar, ignoring those born there. As we talked a man sat and gawped and later he made his approach.

"Niyati?"

"Well. Not any more. It's Rosie now."

"No. You're Niyati. From Tushita."

"Well, I was." The man started to sway and his loose weave smock, that I'm sure he must have been wearing last time we'd met, got caught on the back of my chair. He toppled.

"Oh dear. I'm not centred today. I've lost connection with the earth."

"Well, there's plenty of earth round here, isn't there, although it's all dried up at the moment? I was worried about the cows on the way here. So many of them. It's mainly sheep where I live, but round here it's mainly dairy, isn't it?" I said.

"Why are you worried about the cows?" asked Jan.

"Well, their water. You know. Do they get enough water when it's hot? And then I started worrying about milk. Do they produce different milk, more concentrated, in the summer? Or do they dry up a bit? And, do you think those troughs hold enough for a whole, huge field full of the beasts?"

"It is not your job to worry about the cows." Jan looked seriously concerned, "Have you read Byron Katie yet? *Loving What Is*."

"Er, No actually Jan. I've had enough of all that stuff now, if I'm really honest. I just, you know, get on with it. Live."

"Well, you don't, do you? You're living the cows' lives

171

rather than your own. That's their business; they are perfectly big enough to worry about their own lives. Your life is your business." I could see this was going to be a fairly arduous two days. Swaying man piped up.

"Yeah. I went to a workshop with Katie. It was amazing. I just saw all my trips, you know. I was ashamed really to see how invasive I was. I'd been really giving my partner a whole load of abuse for having a relationship with my brother when I was away visiting Barry Long in Australia. Then I saw that, hey, I don't want my girlfriend to be with me. I want a mythological construction, a mirage of my partner to be with me. I had been so unloving."

"What's your name?"

"Dhyano."

"Hello, Dhyano. I'm Rosie."

"Hello Niyati."

"How old are you now Dhyano?"

"53."

"So, 53 and you're still visiting gurus? Why don't you stop searching now and enjoy what you've found?"

"Wow. Niyati. Thank you. Thank you so much. I am so fortunate to have run into you today. I'd heard, well, there are rumours. Some said that you'd just dropped out of the search altogether. Other people, more lately, have been telling me you've gone into retreat and that you're, like, really up there now. I can see that. Yeah. What made you come out of retreat and to Glastonbury?"

"Well. Do you fancy a lemonade? I'll tell you some stories."

"Wow. I'm really torn now. Wow. Look, I've got to go really. I'm going now, I'm a bit late for, I've got an emotional rebalancing session and I reeaarly need it."

"It was very nice to meet you, er, to see you again, er,

Dhyano."

"Namaste," he said, putting his hands together in front of him as, bowing slightly towards me, he blushed. He shook as he moved away and I thought he was going to topple like one of Teeteryngh's energy targets.

"Yeah, see you Dhyano."

The visit went on in that way for most of its 48 hours. Some of those hours we spent discussing the relative virtues of life with a respectable television mogul, as Jan's had been until very recently, and life with a Shamanistic charlatan who liked ecstasy and fucking. If I were in my seventies, I think I know which I'd choose. The excitement comes with a price. It involves dismantling the integrated set of beliefs necessary for survival in the real world, such as that it's a good idea to pay the gas bill before winter and a bad idea to sleep with your partner's best mate, and replacing these with a sense of guilt about needing things in order to survive, such as gas and freedom from hurt, as well as an absence of pubic lice.

We consulted the Bhagwan Tarot deck, in Jan's case because she needed to unpick some of her confusion about Premda and her part in the betrayal of his trust when Jan had told the third woman to phone him, on her home line, in her house in Pangbourne, of all things, from Australia (he was forever phoning them back) about the other two. She felt that she had been leaking resentment ill-advisedly. I told her that I thought Premda was a cunt but she thought the Bhagwan Tarot might have a more illuminating response. We consulted the deck again, in my case for a bit of a laugh and to find out whether Tom would materialise from cyberspace on Tuesday. I'd decided not to tell Jan about this since I was sure she'd disapprove of trying to find love through miserablemates.com. The cards thought it highly unlikely and Jan's interpretation of their arrangement was that I spent my life concerning myself with others' business. This was a bad thing. I had a bit of an argument with her about this and it turned out that I was also a clinging and overprotective mother who needed to learn to trust and let go, as Delia, her daughter and mother to her grand-daughter, had done.

Luckily, the intense argument was defused when, speaking of the devil as we were, the devilish grand-daughter returned. She was a bit peckish so her mother made her an omelette. Thinking of her nutrition, the mother added a little spinach to the mix but the daughter didn't like spinach so told her mother to fuck off and stop trying to control her and went out to get some chips. When she came back, she had a safety pin through her arm. Very punk. She talked about Dracula and the un-dead and I talked about abuse, boundaries and septicaemia. The bathroom sink smelt of TCP in the morning (god knows where she found it) and there was a safety pin stuck in the soap. I was turning into my mother.

I waited in the high street for quite a long time on Tuesday, checking my mobile phone every five minutes to see if Tom had texted and reading Jan's copy of Byron Katie, which, it was hoped, might save my life just in the nick of time. As I sat, a succession of seekers fell at my feet. News had travelled and the lads came out of the woodwork. I played a game. One brought some incense sticks which I turned down.

"That's really nice of you but I live in the country now and I like to smell the flowers, the grasses and the gentle summer breezes" (and the dung and the chicken shit and the tractor fuel). He bearing incense, his head ringed with fluffy greying hair, which skirted round the edges of his face and more or less all the way round his head save for a widening parting, thought this the most profound thing he had heard for a while, and he beamed. Another had heard I might be able to put him in touch with a man he had done 'marathon-encounter' with in 1975 since he felt he needed a bit of a refresher course in order to deal with back-logged shit over-spilling. I explained that I wasn't local and that I thought the Yellow Pages might be a good place to start if he needed a plumber but it wasn't like that.

"No. Don't you remember me? Niyati? I'm Richard Parkinson. No, not that Parkinson. Blimey. You really have dropped the mind."

"Do you mean Parkie? Are you Parkie from Gavin's 'Richards to Rags', Tushita?"

"Yes. Yes. And that group completely changed my life. I dropped chasing after dreams of fame and stardom and found my own light shining from within, got myself a small shop called Enlightenment. I've been here 25 years now. I sell meditation tapes, gongs and Byron Katie books these days."

"You'll be doing alright for yourself then, round here." It was lost on him.

"Yes. It's an amazing community here. There's a lot of love about."

"Any kids? Wife? Family?"

"No. No children. I was sterilised during sannyas. I don't think I saw you in the commune in India. 1982?"
"There was nobody there."

"No. I didn't know that at the time, when I booked. Nobody said. But it was such a good thing for me, you know. I learnt so much about assumptions and expectations and I've never looked back. It's just recently I've been feeling I need to connect with Gavin's work again. I've got some residual anger covering pain and it has been stopping me from moving forwards since an on-going mind-clearing group I was in broke up." I explained that Gavin was now living in Thailand with a couple of young girls and Parkie thought this was really amazing. I didn't explain that prostitution was demeaning but that the women, being unable to speak Gavin's language, would be spared the consequences of answering back. I realised that such a negative representation of reality would topple me from my pedestal rather more rapidly than I could say 'narcissistic personality disorder'. Instead we exchanged email addresses and he shuffled across the road to his shop for a moment's reflection and a fag.

As Tuesday wore on and the novelty of being an amazing and charismatic seer of all things wonderful wore out, I realised that Tom was not going to turn up. I climbed wearily up the hill, via Parkie's Enlightenment, where the incense cloud peaked at a level likely to incense those who would ban smoking from pubs. Hugs dispensed and suggestions that I return for Byron Katie's visit made, I packed the car and drove away thinking about what it meant to be stood-up by an imaginary friend. I felt a bit of an idiot.

I sang along to Vamoosh's tape, a gift from Parkie, as it squeaked in the ancient cassette player in the car, 'I've been hurt a thousand times, I've been told a million lies but I still believe in love'. Spookily, when I reached the M4, the tape could no longer turn. Perhaps it required the additional energy supplied by the ley-lines. As it snapped, technology intervened, automatically turning to the radio, Johnnie Walker and the drive-time show playing Vince Ray and the Razorbacks.

I wrote to him, of course.

mis:arks

Re: And your blind date is … invisible.

What happened to you then, Mr Spontaneous? I sat there, checking every passing man for a copy of the Observer and a red rose – the nod-nod wink wink, this is the moment when the screen goes back and your blind-date is

…. Seventeen stone and has no dress sense but, nothing. Now, a girl likes to think there's a good reason for her imaginary friend's disappearance and I'm sure you've got a really excellent one tucked up your sleeve.

Drop me a line, if you've time.

R

It seemed reasonable for someone advertised as having calibrated brakes to apply them, with sarcasm. The lowest of low wits, my father said.

mis:arksner

Rosie, Hi.

If you look on Wales.com, you'll see some places near me were evacuated last night following a suspected gas leak. Sorry. Just got in. Can't keep my eyes open. Head down. Sorry. Will write. But there's something I'm finding it difficult to explain

T.

Yeah, right.

As I waited for Tom's explanation the pattern of life resumed its regularity, restlessness giving way to work as exhibition season meetings called me in to earn a living. Sarah and Gillian, disappointed that my cyber friend was even less shaggable than Dave, persuaded me to go to a gig where, a reliable source advised, Sarah's brother-in-law, Fat Graham might just fill the void.

2003

III

The Toaders, the group of old men who wished they had been famous, were playing in Wolverton. Fat Graham, Sarah's brother-in-law, the friend who was destined for more, had said he'd see me there and had gone on ahead with his mandolin. I took my time and chose a dress, far too flimsy for a September gig.

Folkies, old groupies in sweat shirts and jeans, wore novelty T-shirts revealed as the pub heated up, noting their attendance at festivals of varying prestige. Card carrying members wore standard issue black tops, emblazoned with The Toaders' logo. Everyone drank pints of lager.

Down at the old saloon, two half-slatted doors swung away behind me and I took two steps forward to stand, full centre, in my dress as if I were the seam in the rebounding entry gates. A man turned and his gaze bit into raw bones. He twisted to lean on the bar, opening his body towards me, raising one eyebrow, like an arched bow. He picked up his pint with his left hand and nodded to me as he tilted the glass to drink. Incongruously, as the faded navy corduroy round his sleeve slipped with the tilt, a battered Rolex watch stopped my heart. To his right and behind him, Graham screwed something into the base of his guitar and nodded to let me know I'd arrived.

I span in the space between the spectre and the band, pretending to dance, as if he pulled the string of his spinning top. Acquaintances passed between us. Each asked me how the children were and I pretended to be pleased by the gig. Just as Graham broke a string, but quite by chance, the pub's internal shutters failed, against the strain of holding sound inside the venue's decorated windows, swinging backwards to one side and toppling a stack of crisp-boxes, as light flooded the scene. The Toaders covered the embarrassment; I danced and Avalon watched.

As the group struck up the first chords of the second half, I gave up queuing for the Ladies and returned to the scene. Avalon had disappeared.

2003

IV

Days turned to weeks and September shortened days, disturbing the pattern of the weeks. Sarah and Gillian went away to top up their Aerobic tans while I went into recession and risked a mis-risk-click.

Hi Tom
I quite miss my internet stalker.
X R.

And just as if there really is a god, while waiting for my tea to brew, a Joanna Lumley sound-alike announced, "You have mail".

Hi Rosie.
Thank God you're still there. I missed you too. I don't quite know how to tell you this; I've been trying to find a way. It seems so silly, so much from long ago. It is the one thing that needs to be told face to face; but I missed the chance. Forgive me; this explains where I was when I should have been in Glastonbury last month.

I was telling you all about my life and there's some of it I'd rather forget in a way but you know how it is? Some of the moments, when you think about them, some things stay or stick and it seems like we never really move on from these.

I was 18 when I left home and this time instead of my Dad being in the news, because he was always upsetting his neighbours and finding himself locked up, this time I was the one in the papers. I had fallen for a girl in another class at school except that I'd just finished my A levels and she was in the middle of her O level years. Lesley. And she'd fallen for me. Then she fell pregnant. Her Dad would have killed me and I'm sure that, even to this day, he wishes he had got the chance. So we took some money that I still feel really guilty about because I knew then that it was supposed to pay for my Mum's gas and that it would leave her and my brothers short. But we took it anyway.

Well, things didn't turn out right, not at all and although we managed to find somewhere to stay because we met some art students in Reading who were kind and put us up in their back room, I made a terrible mistake. We didn't want anyone to find us you see and we had become national news rather than just local news since Lesley was only 15, and technically I'd abducted her, being 18 and so apparently responsible. Things went from bad to worse but for a while we had each other and some fantastic hopes and dreams of a new life.

One night, we were on our own because the students had gone out to Reading Festival so we had the run of the flat, on this one night. Lesley started bleeding although the baby wasn't due for at least another four months. I'd shied away from anything bloody, I was really hopeless with anything too physical and yet there was just blood, everywhere it seemed. I really didn't know what to do and I handled it really badly. She was haemorrhaging and I knew that I should take her to a hospital but I didn't dare because of course I didn't want to be arrested for paedophilia. It wasn't such a fashionable term then but nevertheless I was with a girl who I shouldn't have been with and I was too weak to do what I knew I should.

The night wore on and I thought that if she just lay down in the bed and kept her feet above her head, a bit as I had had to when I used to have nose bleeds as a kid, then somehow the baby would remain lodged where it should and everything would be alright. Long story short, it wasn't and when I woke, lying next to her in the back of a seedy flat I was drenched in her blood and the poor girl had died in the night. Died. In this day and age. I just hadn't considered the possibility. And I can't say anything more than that now and I'm sorry, Rosie, that I have said too much here already. But I felt I had to really, to give you the fuller picture instead of just hinting all the time that there was some babe in the sixth form who'd been nice enough to kiss me. It wasn't like that and I really wish, of course I wish, it had been.

I'll never forget the journey home. We were two sides of the bus aisle with my Dad falling over on my Mum and then leaning on the window and my Mum just sitting there, the other side of the aisle from me, holding my hand with our arms swinging in the gap. It was surreal really because of course my Mum and Dad had to come although it would have been better if my Dad had stayed at home. He spent three days in Reading in the Butts Centre getting drunk and trying to persuade someone to let him play snooker while my Mum and I went through all the police interviews and the formalities, trying to stay out of the way of Lesley's brother and her Dad. It was enough that she had died and my Mum knew I would have been happy enough to surrender myself, really, to let her father beat me up. I wanted to go with her. No one would even arrest me. I don't know why. Everyone else I knew suffered rejection, and that awful competition that went on for them to keep their girlfriends from running off, was the one I so wanted to be in and I suddenly found myself wishing I had died rather than remain to face this awful music, dreadful, awful, and the consequences. On top of that, I'd lost everything. The girl I loved. My baby. The dream. I didn't think Northampton would ever be able to cover the past over. That's when I had to go away. I was right, don't you think?

On that Tuesday, when I was supposed to meet you at 2pm, I thought I could make it; I thought I could you know but that Tuesday was the anniversary and, every time, every year so far, when the day comes around again, as it does, I have been to Northampton to sit on the bench where Lesley and I first kissed. So I went, earlier then the dawn, but I sat too long and I just couldn't get to Glastonbury on time. And then somehow, I couldn't tell you this.

Thank you, Rosie. You make my head turn again. Thank you. I hope this is not too much.
X T

Dear Tom

I met a couple once, at a bus stop, long before I should have been meeting people at bus stops. They were hitching through our village and I invited them in for a cup of tea. (They'd been there for a few hours and no one would stop because they were tattered and punkish. A real coup for a middle-class girl.) He was a bit older than me, maybe 18 at a pinch but terribly naïve, shy underneath and she was, they said, 16 and a lot more worldly wise than I was. They were on the run and they needed somewhere to stay but they thought Reading would be better than Streatley-on-Thames. My parents were away in the South of France. They were in the habit of leaving me. Once I got to 16 they thought they could risk it.

These kids, Tim and Kathy they called themselves, had nothing at all. A large canvas bag, a duffle bag and each other. So I said they could stay. They had a bottle of my Dad's wine while I cooked: pork chops, under the grill, with sour cream and paprika, some spinach. It was what my mother would have done. I only remember because I only ever cooked twice as a kid and I did the same dish both times. Anyway, they had a bath and set up home for the night in the lounge. We had plans but in the morning, they'd gone. They left a note saying they had had to leave. They'd taken £5 out of my bag, because they had to, but they'd send it in the post. They never did.

Later, a month or so, there was a huge headline in the Reading Mercury about two kids who'd gone missing from the North. At least I think it was the North. I'd never been anywhere much. And we were supposed to ring the local police station if we'd seen them at all. By then, my parents were home and I knew I'd get in trouble if I said. So I didn't and over the years, through not saying, I guessed I'd imagined it all.

R. x

Rosie.

I owe you a fiver. When can we meet? Tom. X

The extraordinary coincidence inspired me to agree to a

picnic, in Streatley-on-Thames, where, long ago, we had met where the red kites turn in the sky. Waiting for the reunion, we advanced to mis-androidpy. Here, you could click on a range of colours and tones to flood the screen to match the mood of the conversation; we kept ours on beige, except for the occasional mishap. We, Tom and I, were represented by animated cartoon characters which produced speech bubbles as we typed. His was a beige man, with a beard, in chinos, with green shoes and a baseball cap turned backwards. Mine was an Alison Moyet look-alike. I needed to make myself sound a bit less past it than I felt. I asked him about drugs.

He and Lesley had had speed. I remembered because it had frightened me. Later, I'd noticed, therapists I'd met had all at some point been addicted to nasty drugs, like heroin but ordinary wannabes seemed to stick to something you could grow in a flower pot or something that made you want a hug. I'd delivered my son and daughter to a rave. Rob had been ungracious, leaping from the car without a nod of thanks, in his leopard skin tights with his boxers on the outside and green eye shadow completing the look: strange for someone so homophobic. Freya had sent me a text.

Big up to your generation for this culture, Mum.
You're so cool.
Thank you thank you thank you.
I love you sooooo much :) x

My mother, unable to accept that I would willingly take my children to something I had been forced to leave home to attend had scoured the Radio Times for a clue. She'd said,

"Oh look. It goes on until midnight or later perhaps but they're having a big build up till 11pm when they've got Fergie. Fergie. What the hell's happening to royalty? They think they've got to, well, you know. She was no good from the start that one. Bad news. If you can't beat 'em, join them. I don't know." I was ashamed of it really. But I thought that, perhaps, if enough people took nice drugs, the world would change.

Tom, ever the realist, explained as chino-boy-green-shoe man walked backwards and forwards across the screen: All through the eighties, people were taking Es at football matches. They thought there'd been a miracle because all the fights stopped but it wasn't a miracle. They thought their systems had worked. It wasn't systems either. It was the Es. The crowd were all loving each other.

Alison Moyet frowned: I'm just waiting for people to think to themselves, afterwards, 'Right! That was nice. Let's be more relaxed, let's be nicer', share that perfectly ordinary love in our perfectly ordinary lives.

Shoe-beard-man-boy blushed, spyware reading a thesaurus: You're such. You're romantic. I'm sorry. I'm a pessimist, maybe. I don't know really, you know what I mean? Life's not like that, is it?

Moyet, moony eyed: Yes. I know. I can pretty it up.

Chino-shoe-boy, throwing his cap in the air: And you're going to start putting MDMA in the water system are you?

Alison, turning orange: I thought that might be a good idea; perhaps we could do an experiment and put it in the water system of one village but not the next; to gamble a placebo effect to find out whether people really have lost the knack of being content entirely of their own volition. For a laugh.

We navigated through the hippies' drugs, to white poison; heroin, vodka speed and cocaine.

Chino-Tom, holding his cap in his hands: The trouble was, for my contemporaries, the punks, the stuff they –

we – I – was taking. Not like the hippies, all on dope, so sleepy about everything, I suppose. Speed we took. Heroin, even, yes, eventually. It burnt into my friends. They just weren't my friends anymore, in both senses. And, you know, you can imagine, it left a hole through the middle of us. We, it, um, it burnt us out too soon. And it didn't really help that we had Thatcher come along then. You know what that meant, we all do of course. Stewart talks about it; he kept an eye on Mum. It was dreadful in our house because my mum, you know she was out working all the time but it wasn't enough. God this sounds tragic but, once we'd left, the boys, and there was just Mum left with Dad, that was when Thatcher sort of jumped on the wagon, chucking her weight around, my Mum went to pieces, so my Dad got, you know, shaken off the wagon, if you know what I mean. Everything was closed except the pub.

Me and my girlfriend – the second one, the Vibrators, my wife Slash in fact – second love – we were, you know, off our faces on something-or-other for most of that period. Drink in my case, mostly. Slash was there when Lesley and the baby weren't. I got into the Vibrators; the drink and the drugs, washing up all day, wiping tables, scamming tips and trying to keep up. It took a lot of Vodka, and the rest. I had a break, once; went to a sort of rehab centre for a while but it all started again. I just kept ending up back in Wales. My Mum. She came to live in Wales. That helped.

Alison Moyet bends her head, curtsey like: Yes.

Chino: The first time, I was only 18. I kept it together for a while, and at 22, I thought I'd left it all behind. I got in with a new crowd but even that went terribly wrong; left me hanging, up to no good and I finished up in hospital in the end. Mental. I was off the drugs; drinking now and then but it was life that finally went for me, and.

Alison Moyet looks as if she is waiting for applause.

Green-shoe-chino-bearded-man-boy: Weird, strange, coincidentally, I wound up in a long stay psychiatric unit in 1977. I'd only been away from Wales for three years. I used to say four. Four since I'd left home. Slash had somehow managed to keep a part-time job as a ward orderly. I found myself back in Wales, in the same hospital she worked in. We tried to make a go of it. Had a couple of kids.

Moyet nods.

Chino boy-man skips: But. Well. It's. (Another skip.) Chino resumes: Oh, well, you know, we just fell into it again and, you know. Every day. I started drinking, never got back on the drugs though.

Alison Moyet opens her hand and a flower falls.

Chino: It says something for the rehab stuff: even though I went mad, I stayed off the bad shit. It took the edge off, vodka, her white powders, whatever, until we found we were living on the bloody edge. True to say, I have to admit, well, you know, it fucked us up.

Chino-green-shoe-boy-man looks at his watch: We really can't spend our lives typing.

As Alison Moyet and Hat-shoe-beard-boy-man left the screen, they turned their backs and walked away, looking round to smile and wave wide arms as the page reverted to home.

Fat Graham and his instruments, living a simple life, wanted to offer me more but I'd had longer now to decide about cyber space. Tom's revelations had somehow drawn me in. I'd have to break it to Graham; there was a gig in a week or two and

Ghatoh, last seen looking as if she were a beached whale which had crawled onto a sofa post sterilisation in Pune, had emailed and was coming to stay. I found it strange. There was also a party coming up after that to celebrate Jan's 70th birthday, a re-run of the reunion in the Spring, when Premda had come, stirring visions and a sense of unease. I felt a need to establish something of my own without such reference to my past. Under plan A, I decided, I'd go to Streatley and meet Tom and, all being as I expected it to be, I'd skip the gig and let Ghatoh set the town alight without me.

2003

V

Tom was feeling optimistic since his house was now renovated and sold, subject to the whims of a surveyor, and his new life as a free agent seemed a closer possibility than before. He had or would soon have taken delivery of his new mobile-home. He and I arranged to meet at the bus stop in Streatley-on-Thames in late September, 2003. There I waited by the bus-shelter which had been torn down and re-erected, without the graffiti, to make way for a small brass sculpture commemorating an avid twitcher who'd enjoyed the view of the hill. I had written there, once, 'I love Andrew Hunt R.T.' and he had written, 'Buga Off' which had caused a few wry smiles. Thirty or forty years on, the only notices concerned planning and plotting. The residents of my childhood home had grown greedy and appealed to the village to accept their proposal that a five-bedroom house, with parking, should stand where once I had tethered my broomstick pony, his nose a sock nestled into a bucket of airy hay, beside the composted mulch where I had first found love and Patrick. I took down the address of the planning office and composed an objection as I watched cars slow, stop and start from the traffic lights.

A gleaming Mercedes house on wheels cruised looking for a place to stop but finding no space between Land Cruisers the driver, a woman in her late forties perhaps, long thin and with ravaged arms bent round the horizontal steering wheel, scowled and moved on. I lingered, hoping for Tom. At 2.30pm when he was already half an hour late, a text.

I'm sorry. I can't.

I swung the Peugeot onto the road, turning back to retrace the path trodden twenty years ago, thirty, when Tom was an old boy and Lesley, now gone, was still here and pregnant. Driving out to where the Ridgeway began, all along the once dusty paths stood the homes of the rich, and beyond these, the untamed open sky. I stopped the car and spread a blanket on the ground, sipping fizzy apple from just one of the two champagne flutes brought along, tribute to a wedding feast.

And the red kites soared, possessing the pale blue fading depths of an early twenty-first century's sky. I'd asked Graham, on a break in a gig,

"Would you swap lives or keep the one you've had? You know, have mine instead of yours?"

"I don't think that's such a great choice, is it Rosie? What about, I don't know, you know, um, if you offered me, I don't know, Sting's life, I've always thought it'd be quite nice to be Sting. But I don't know really. Perhaps, you know, the devil you know, perhaps that's, I don't know."

"I'm not saying mine is better." I hoped I'd not made him uneasy.

"Me neither. My mother was always going on about, 'when you get to my age' and now I'm sort of, I don't know. We seem to be sort of made up as we go along."

"I'd swap mine with a bird. A big bird though. Red kite, perhaps."

The Berkshire Downs rolled away and I thought about long hot summer days that seemed to go on for ever. I thought about Patrick Connor, my childhood's end in love. Once, my friend Lizzie and I had packed a small green canvas bag with sandwiches and Robinson's lemon barley, leaking from a tin thermos, and set out for an adventure. It had seemed another world and coming across a shed in the woods we had imagined ourselves caught up in intrigue as we sat at another's makeshift table, abandoned, and pictured an ape-man regression returning to find trespassers at home. All those warnings about eating porridge that didn't belong to you and being fattened up in gingerbread houses rolled into the impression to scare us home.

Later, when I should have been at choir practice we went there again, to the empty sky. Lizzie and I toying with the Andrew Hunts of this world who'd burrowed into a haystack in a barn to create a four-walled enclosure from the bales. There we whiled away the Wednesday evenings while Lizzie learnt about snogging and I worried that Pete Smith would burn us to death with his cigarette in the dry tinder furnace that hid us.

Still further into the recesses of time there was a memory, passing here, of some longhaired public school boys with a transit van who'd painted it psychedelic and driven off only to break down on their way to the east. There, inside that van, the otherworldly adventures took them, instead, to a place where everything was conjoined in the dancing colours of the universe unleashed by LSD: a horror when the family doctor was called to intercept a bad trip.

I ate the chocolate cake I'd made, a deep, moist concoction, steamed in a Bain Marie, with 77% chocolate, sugar, eggs and double cream oozing into the crevices of a ridged picnic bowl from a set which fitted neatly into a hamper, strapped in, a present from a grateful artist, Christmas, '94.

As the evening thermals carried the red kites to roost, again, in Aldworth, I retraced my steps, hurrying home and struggling to appreciate Dolly Parton on Fat Graham's educative compilation cassette.

Dawn's shards criss-crossed my face, as if it were steak in a griddle pan, as Freya burst into my room.

"An internet bloody. I don't. I mean? You make me puke. Really. Look. I live here. I wasn't snooping. I didn't do anything wrong, you know. I live here."

"So do I."

"So you can leave it out about the boundaries."

"I was going to."

"It's you. You can't be trusted on the net."

"Yes."

"I was just saying that, at your age, you know, Christ. God, you know. How would you feel if, like, you. It's disgusting."

"I think that's a bit rich. He's a nice guy you know. Tom. Well, I think he is. I'd know if he hadn't had his van nicked. I'm, well, I'm not just for the bloody chores, you know."

"Oh, right. Yeah. You just start going on about the fucking cleaning, washing, cooking and your poor me routine now. What fucking van? Don't tell me you believe all that shite. Fucking mental. You're not bloody stable. You need to get your hormones looked at. It'll be that. That's what's doing it. Christ. You're a funny age now, love."

"You're probably right but I still think I could, perhaps, do something other than evening classes through these long winter evenings. No?"

"Track record. Let's have a look shall we. Now let's see. Working forwards. We'll do it this way. Starting with my dad. Well. I expect even he thinks he deserves some kind of an award for parenting skills. You, on the other hand, well, there it is. Piece de résistance, having worn out all the rest of this godforsaken town's has-beens you produce Fat Graham – and god knows how many others' lives you're trying to ruin. Now, the internet, for fuck's sake. The internet. Not content with finding all the local nutters. The internet. The world-wide-fucking-net. The world's your fucking oyster. What do you do? So you think it might be a good idea to get some fucking nutter off the net. What do you want, a round of applause or something?"

"I'm sorry." I grinned. "Look. I screwed up. Quite a lot. Granted. I am sorry. Dreadfully so. But, we escaped. Got away. My mistake, sure, and yes, I have been on rather a lot of misguided dates over the years and the latest, I agree, Fat Graham is a git, I agree, but I don't see why I shouldn't, you know. Get on with the rest of my life."

"Oh, yeah. Right. Funny that. What the fuck sort of life do you think you're going to find hanging about with sad losers who have to use the world wide dot fucking net to get a dirty postcard (please tell me you didn't ask him on a fucking picnic) off some sad old woman who ought to know better?"

She slammed the door, leaving me scouring the pockets of my recent lucky find from the hospice shop for a packet of Rizlas and some Amber Leaf. I got in the car and sped off to the garage. I'd forgotten my wallet. Under the seat, the driver's side, I found: half a, I guessed prawn, sandwich; three scratch-cards; a biro; a book about the mid-west, from Graham, to encourage me to enjoy country-folk which I hadn't seen since the exhaust fell off; and some Golden Virginia, the dregs. I parked outside home and smoked all there was left in the packet, watching my daughter go from room to room, slamming doors and ignoring 'The Darkness' howling from an upstairs room, mine, as loud as the Sony-music-centre-circa-1987 would go. I crept into the house and up the stairs, lying low until the tape came to an end.

I tottered on egg shells, unable to do much more than rationalise my shoe collection: taking a bag-full to the hospice shop and coming home, via the bakers and on to the factory outlet in the high street, with some £10 knee highs and some patent click-heels, to sort t-shirts into summer, winter and underwear piles and to panic about the dearth of decent knickers.

I put the kettle on. There in the kitchen, waiting for me, memories on the notice board were hidden beneath an offering from Freya. A new, A4 print out from the net. Someone had auctioned their life. You could get the whole thing: job; house; friends even. The starting price was way beyond my price range.

Freya, with flowers for me, watched me pour the water into the pot. She smiled at the chocolate muffins.

"High street?" (about the flowers).

"Tesco. Budgens?" (about the chocolate muffins).

"Bakers."

"Cup of tea?"

"Coffee."

"Sorry."

"Me too. Sorry." We hugged. "Chill, Mum, what's the matter?"

"Nothing. I was just thinking about how much of me is in you and if."

"God, Mum."

"No, you know. How much of you comes from nature

and how much of that is from me. Is that the same question?"

"Well, duh, Mum?"

"I mean."

"70s. Gurus. All that baloney. Never did you any good. It's about time, Mum, isn't it?"

"What?"

"Get a Life."

2003

VI

After so many years - I hadn't seen her since 1981 - it was bizarre that Ghatoh should choose that particular weekend, the first of October, for her visit. I had told her I'd discovered the pleasure in ordinary life, playing the part of the zany-arty-lefty-single-parent, living in a field, in a village relegated to suburbia with the growth of Milton Keynes. Ghatoh was impressed that I'd worked my way up in the art world, doing practical things for artists and, buoyed up, she expected the Folk scene to stand in for Romance. Drawing to a close at the end of September, the annual music festival resurrected for its climactic aural orgy and, anticipating a bang, Ghatoh came to immerse herself in country-folky-rock.

Fat Graham, my friend who was the other idea, was to open the night, with The Toaders who would set the tone. He was, this time, quite lost in his business since it fell to him to play Master of Ceremonies and make sure that all went to plan. He had to manage a succession of acts, playing through the night, in a vast open barn behind the pub, and in support of the headline act, Kent Du Chaine, who had travelled all the way from the mid-west, USA, with Led Bessie, his steel guitar. In honour of this effort, an anonymous donor had procured from Marshall's a state of the art sound-desk. It could only be operated by a trained engineer, the benefactor, who would be thanked later on. I bought Ghatoh a ticket and left her to sit alone on a hay bale while I ran errands for Graham.

The box-office was a rickety table set across the entrance to the barn. Once fully paid up, revellers were stamped bright green on the back of the hand. Numbered programmes, with promise of a meal for the lucky winner of the prize draw, had to be advertised and sold. The pile on the desk, running low, was to be re-stocked from fresh programmes tied in string and stored in a plastic box to the side of the barn, out of sight. Being in charge, I took a blunt knife to the twine of a new bundle out of view. A voice and I looked up.

"Try this." He held a multi-tool, a blade prepared.

"Avalon."

"If you like."

"I - "

"I hoped you'd be here. Dancing tonight?"

"Avalon. Oh Avalon. I." A Toader, a fiddle player, approached from the car park at the back.

"Alright Rosie? You on programmes?" and nodded at the man with the knife. "That's a big one, mate." They nodded and leer-jeered as men do. Avalon sliced through the parcel's binding.

"There, Rosie. Rosie. Rosie. Lovely name."

"And, you're?"

"Call me Malachi, or Mal, or Key."

"Malachi. Lovely. Back to your roots?"

"Do you have time, Rosie? Can we?"

"Just give me five minutes, ok. Wait for me, please, wait

for me this time. Will you?" He pulled a packet of Lambert and Butler from his back pocket, turned a bale towards the long-day-late-sun and swilled lager in the bottom of the glass. I asked,

"Drink?"

"No, look. You do what you've got to do. I'll get the drinks. I'm on Carlsberg. What's yours, Rosie Rose?"

"Stella."

"Half?"

"A pint, if you don't mind."

"Grand."

It had been a particularly well-attended season of gigs in the locality that summer and before the week-long music festival. People had come to be reunited with old friends, as Ghatoh declared she had come to me, and others had come on professional business, either as sponsors for advertising or in support of charity. At least, I understood that to be the case.

In the barn behind the pub the week-long festival for mid-life cripples in search of Romance drew to an end. The start of its long closing night, with the first chords of The Toaders' opening song, straining out and across the car-park to the fields, was underway as I delivered the programmes to Fat Graham's mate, Ian. I checked that Ghatoh, who'd come for the dancing, was still in the barn. She was looking forward to Kent du Chaine and Led Bessie at the end of the night and happy to sit there and wait while I helped and ran errands. Hopefuls and has-beens played loudly on the stage as mid-life divorcees re-shuffled themselves on the dance floor and my friend Graham kept everything in order.

I crept to the shortening-day's evening-light and Avalon-now-Malachi's bale outside. This time, he'd waited, with the drinks, the grand pint of Stella and a drink for himself; I marvelled that he'd stayed.

We could not say a word.

He tried to look away but we drew close. Kissing, still a trace of a cigarette in his mouth, Carlsberg vapour gently dredging my senses, his hand held my face close-tight to his; I felt he had nothing else in his mind or in his being other than kissing me.

I spent the night running like the wind from his hold, to the hay-bale-chitter-chatter-make-a-noise, "Are you alright Ghatoh? Good." Back again, faster still to Avalon. Malachi. A touch of the hand; a stroke of the back; a light brush of the face; a look and a knowing. I had settled for adrenaline with Gavin. Love, just of late, had fallen to the mundane, workable even; the sort of love you might just get with a Graham or any of the mid-life-misery-guts who vied for a bit on the side. Malachi-Avalon re-kindled a fire.

A synthetic twilight-dawn threw a dusty veil over the sound-desk, tight shards of morning breaking through skylights as, to frenzied expectation, Kent Du Chaine took to the stage. Friendly Graham, with a postcard prompt, welcomed him and urged that we all applaud, "Give it up" a little more "Large" than we thought we could once for Kent from the Mid West of the U. S. of A., and then again for,

"Michael, is that right? No. Sorry. Mal. It is Malachi. I can't read my own writing here! So, let's give it up for Malachi Murphy of Sound Events, for what we're about to receive. Give it up, for Malky, for setting this small town, down-town home, on fire with full-blown, rock the night away, Marshall accessorized, professional sound."

The barn, on Stella-cum-Carlsberg more than genuine joie de vivre, raised the roof as Avalon, lately Malachi, Mal, Key, Malky, assumed the position, driving the sound-desk full-frontal to the stage. Kent Du Chaine charmed the ladies with a gyrating grin while Fat Graham, moving to claim that which he hoped soon to call his, leant 17 stone of possession on my shoulders and clamped his hand vice-like round my waist. I was held in suspension, 18 inches from Malachi's sound-desk-altar, tribute to life.

Ghatoh, boogying to my right said,

"That sound man. Does he remind you of anyone Niyati?"

"Rosie."

"Sorry."

"You what?" I hedged.

"Oh, it's just that I, no. Silly. Forget it. I forget how big the world is sometimes."

"So do I."

Graham was too busy packing-up and being congratulated to wonder where I'd gone and I slipped round the corner as the night grew sticky with upturned limey lager and unhappy hopefuls wooing their prey with kebabs. Ghatoh, claiming fat-leg sweat-rub rash, had gone on ahead for an amuse bouche, courtesy of my fridge. Avalon-Malachi unplugged leads, rolling cables, holding neat coils in plastic clip locks, pushing his dark hair from his eyes, the incongruous Rolex rattling a wrist, as I watched from our hay-bale, through a crack in the barn, keeping an eye on his van, emblazoned with a logo, 'Sound Events'.

Avalon-Malachi told me that he would be in Europe for the rest of the summer and that he'd not be back again; he travelled; he didn't want to stay. He played me Bob Seger, bouncing off the four metal van walls of the musical box, to tell me we had the night; so I stayed, helpless in his lair. In there, in the van, speakers strapped to internal walls with orange straps and stainless clips, we rotated in each other's arms until the back doors flew open and the spare can, rocking against us, clattered onto the concrete road beyond.

Graham, acting on grape-vine news, had reverted to advertising himself, 'A big friendly bear', through the Observer's lonely hearts, and some time after my night with Malachi-Avalon in his van, as he followed the birds southwards playing songs, Ghatoh and Graham lunched in Soho, toasting The Observer and enjoying the coincidence of their advertisements for love.

2003

VII

There was no doubt that Premda could be a catalyst for change, even as late as 2003. Take Jan, for example. She, at very nearly 70, had revelled in the reunion of the commune in the spring and it could be argued that she was the only one of those dredged up from the past to attend who really took to the exercise like a duck to water, joining in ecstatic dance to The Temptations just as if she had done the dynamic meditation that very morning. And to celebrate she'd organised a return match, planned in honour of her seventieth birthday and to celebrate exchange of contracts on her marital home, the country pile and party venue.

I'd arrived, fashionably late, with a huge Wedgwood platter plastered with sticky lemon puddings. Premda, who'd settled in earlier that afternoon, procuring some weed from some ex-junkies he'd met in Pangbourne and some delicious off-cuts from a high class fishmongers looking over the Thames, meditated over a cauldron of bubbling fish-guts on the Aga. His forgotten daughter, last seen at the top of the pyramid of children peering through the skylight in the barn during the Bodhidharma therapy group, stood beside him with her terrified fiancé, as Premda stirred the brew and Jan's own respectably liberal children fussed over a cake. It had all seemed to be going quite well.

Jan was an old friend and patron of Tushita and had been since she'd met Premda and Luminosah when a van they'd been using for their enterprising window-cleaning business slipped from its parking space, its hand-brake failing, and into the back of Jan's shiny new black Mercedes. Premda and Luminosah had followed Jan home to her secluded bohemian mansion where they'd given her a price for the windows. The windows had offered Jan a glimpse of life as it was led by normal healthy neurotics struggling to break free from repression and, within a week, she had signed up to do a 48 hour encounter marathon, with Gavin at Tushita.

In the marathon of 1976 Jan had revealed that although it was really terribly sad that her husband's heart had recently failed under the pressure of life as a banker, she felt nonetheless liberated by his death and ripe for adventure. Yet, life being life, Jan had fallen prey to yet another binding commitment pretty soon after the marathon and time had passed much as it had done beforehand. It was uncanny that Premda's visit, and the commune reunion of 2003, coincided with the death of Jan's second husband. She was, yet again, poised on the dry bank of the past; wrung with seven years spent nursing her ailing husband, Jan had thought she would never have sex again.

The night closed around the happy guests, united at Jan's table; Premda's fish stew was both a hit and a miss; he liked it tremendously and there would be plenty left for tomorrow. My sticky puddings and Jan's gooey cheeses dispatched, we shuffled to Bob Marley, Barry White and Marvin Gaye, for old times' sake. Premda managed to reassure his daughter and her man, who were both stoned, that time and space were an illusion and thus he had not neglected his parenting for 25 years after all, and Jan set off fireworks in celebration of renewal, healing and love. At midnight, Jan claimed that a headache took her to bed and Premda passed out on the grate. In fact, nothing much happened at all. I snuck away, driving across the night.

The following day was Sunday and, against my better judgement, I had agreed that Tom could come to lunch. I had forgiven him on the understanding that his van had let him down and so I'd suffered disappointment in Streatley. Third time lucky, perhaps. Unbeknown to me, Rob, who had offered to draw up a fitness-plan for his teacher in return, had agreed that Fat Graham could teach him how to play the guitar; Rob had found a bargain Spanish acoustic model, complete with strings, in the Oxfam shop and hoped it might enhance his pulling power. I was just about to find a third cup of coffee and start the long process of transforming my complexion when the doorbell rang.

"It's ok. It's for me," called Rob, thundering down the stairs. I was horrified when I saw who'd just arrived.

"Graham. I didn't expect to see you at this time on a Sunday morning. God. Excuse the, well, excuse the state of me."

"You look marvellous. Bohemian chic." I was wearing leggings, slippers in the form of two small elephants and a Chinese embroidered smoking-jacket belonging to my grandfather. "And it's not you I'm here to see," explained Graham. "We're going to see if we can't train Rob up for the band." Rob broke out in a sweat.

"Blimey, Graham. I'm not sure about that. I was hoping

205

to learn a few chords first."

"Sorry, mate. Didn't mean to frighten you. Shall we get on?" They locked themselves into the front room. It was 11am and my internet date was due in an hour and a half.

I lurked, dressing in a casual mix of tight crisp denim with an understated silk t-shirt as I tried to ignore the jovial banter of an old man trying to get to me via the kids. Rob's twanging and some show-off demonstration from Graham accompanied my panic as I nonchalantly tossed a complicated salad and marinated the artichoke. At noon, the doorbell rang and Rob flew from his peripatetic exercise to see who had arrived: a representative of the residents' association with a petition. We all signed it, even Graham who, moving to follow the petition down the road, shook Rob's hand and winked at me to tell me that he'd gone.

"What a wanker," said Rob. "What have I done? Will you tell him, Mum, or have I got to break my hand to stop him trying to teach me music?"

"Er. . . I. . . Are you not working today? I thought you and Freya were out at that silver wedding do, on the washing up?"

"No. It was cancelled." A roar as a van screeched to a halt outside. "But I'm off up to the Booths' now so I'll see you tomorrow. Ok?" and he left as I strained my neck to see the origin of the screeching brakes. Not Tom.

12.15 pm. I regained my composure. Thank god Tom had a habit of being late; I assumed he would come, this third time. I checked the kitchen, messing it up a bit. There was an accident with the fruit compote at 12.30 and I had to raid Freya's bedroom for the hairdryer, to dry the 'vanished' stain, rather than risk changing into a t-shirt that clung to my stretch marks. 'Free Love' didn't look so good if you held it up against the varicose veins. I spent twenty minutes curtain twitching and rearranging notices about exciting family events on the cork board for optimum effect.

I was flushing the loo when the doorbell rang and the fluster ruined my off-hand composure. I'd arranged with Sarah of unshaggable Dave that I would send a text message with marks out of ten for first impressions. Luckily, since registering with miserablemates, he'd told me that he'd lost the beard but the man at the door still took me by surprise.

"Avalon."

"Hi Rosie. You look gorgeous."

"Av, sorry, Malachi. What are you doing here? You'd better come in." Tom, now already half an hour late having promised faithfully to turn up and on time, had competition. I felt I was about to appear in something akin to a Brian Rix farce and decided to hide Avalon-cum-Malachi outside. I led him through the house to sit on a bench in the garden, flicking the switch on the kettle as we passed. "I'm. . . I'm a bit distracted. We may have another visitor in a minute."

"Well, I . . ."

"Oh no. Don't worry. He's even more unreliable than you. Tea or coffee, or would you like a beer?" As I heaped three spoons of sugar into the Nescafe, my hand shaking, I showered the shining lids of storage jars lined up on the side in a mist of fine white powder. "It's a lovely day. Perhaps we should be on the Pimms," I said, joining Malachi in the garden. He took my hand.

"I've something to tell you Rosie. I." The doorbell.

"Oh god. Sorry. Um."

"I'll go."

"No. Hang on." It was a deaf man selling tea towels in aid of blind dogs for the hearing. I showed the tea towel to Malachi. "In lieu of an internet stalker, a tea towel."

"Sorry?"

"Ah. Well. I too have a confession but you go first. I think I've probably been led a merry dance by some lesbian from Luton pretending to be a hairy man from Wales."

"No." He looked me straight in the face as if he thought I couldn't be that stupid.

"Yes, I know. How stupid am I? I joined -"

" - miserablemates.com" he said.

"Yes. Not you too?"

"Fraid so. And I haven't been entirely honest." Tom grimaced.

"No one expects honesty online." The doorbell again. "Oh my god. Look. It's not really the day for this, Avalon. Malachi. I think I'm going to have to ask you to leave." I left him in the garden as I moved to open the front door, checking in the mirror on the way that no accidental blemish of lipstick or compote remained. The door whined on its hinge. Another surprise.

"   Rosie. Sorry. God, you look stunning. Are you on your own now only I think I left my plectrum in the lounge?"

"Oh. Graham. Come in and have a look but I've got someone with me, I'm afraid. A friend. Um. An old friend. Err. We go back decades."

"Sorry Rosie. Your lad's ever so good on the old ghee-tar you know. Look. I can see it from here. On the arm of the sofa. I'll just get that and be gone. Alright?" Graham winked yet again.

"Fine. And by the way, seeing as you're here. Rob doesn't want any more lessons and I know about you and Ghatoh so you've not got a chance."

"Fair enough. Mind, I guessed as much, oh pot and kettle, when I saw his van outside."

"What?"

"Don't play the innocent." He slid his plectrum into a

special pocket just inside his brown leather wallet and turned away.

Returning to Malachi, on the bench in the garden I said,

"Not the close shave I was expecting but he's a bitter man." Secretly I was quite enjoying the coincidence of being pursued, albeit in a low key fashion, by two men with the thrilling promise of a third, if Tom was as good as his word. I planned to keep one or two behind the sofa and fly from room to room, hiding the truth as in 'Sleuth'.

"Who's the bitter man? Surely, that wasn't someone I know?" Malachi had not been able to see the voice from where he sat.

"No. Well yes but no. Although funnily enough, I went to a big reunion last night. Premda was there. He's been in England for six months; it's his first visit since Tushita and it's been making me feel quite weird. I thought I'd got away from all that and now there's you too. But that was just Graham. Graham just came round. The man from the barn? He was giving my son guitar lessons but that's come to an end. Came for his capo or something. Anyway. I was expecting someone else."

"Yes, I know," said Malachi.

"Sorry. I must seem very rude. It looks to me like he's not bloody coming. Internet. I've been duped. You were saying, about miserablemates. You'd been a bit wicked. Well we all are aren't we? I don't tell the truth. You can't be as bad as this bloke Tom. He just seems to make it all up."

"Well. I do live in Wales."

"Did I tell you he was from Wales then? Or? Oh my god. How do you know about Wales?" I stood up, moving away and creeping towards the apple-tree to the far right of the bench where he sat. The hand gripping my coffee cup seemed suddenly translucent, energy coursing through me in waves as my grasp failed, spraying coffee in an arc over late summer roses.

"Rosie. Please. I'm so sorry."

"You're sorry? For stalking me and tracking me down, first in a pub and now in my home? And now I find - Oh my god, you've been hacking into my computer. What else do you know?"

"Only what you told Tom. I'm sorry."

"Sorry? You're sorry? You even know his bloody name. Sorry? How did you get into Tom's account for god's sake?"

"No. It's me. I'm Tom. I've been trying to say."

"We. Why? We spent a night: you told me you were off on tour and that; you carried on writing; you've had me driving left right and centre; I've even been to fucking Glastonbury."

"I'll go. I'm sorry. A big mistake."

"Mistake? None of this was an accident. You turn up here; you sleep with me under one name; stalk me on the net; creep around pubs; get me to confide."

"I wanted to tell you. I've always wanted to tell you about my life. I didn't like it that you thought I was just some failed therapist with no excuse for getting it wrong. I thought you'd understand. I'm sorry. I think I should go."

"Oh yeah. And what about that crap about the poor lost baby. I told you, didn't I? Or was that in a group? About my punk hitchers at the bus stop. And you used it. You used that to draw me in? You devious. I. What else?" The shaking took hold; my teeth chattered together as I drew the cardigan's two halves across each other binding them with my arms to keep safe.

"No. It's true. Please. All I've told you, all I wanted you to know. It's true."

"But. I don't know what to believe. Is that the bell

again?" I left him there and wandered into the house, knowing that I was no longer waiting for my internet caller but still expecting a man from Wales to turn up. Upstairs in the bathroom mirror, my eyes were bloodshot blue and the crease dividing the left side from the right of my forehead seemed to mirror the front of the cardigan, now buttoned, as if I were a pasty about to split and spill its contents for analysis. Hanging over the banister was a huge cream coloured IKEA throw, washed and ready to be folded away for next year's festival season. I grabbed it, throwing it over both shoulders and catching it in two fists across my torso as if my hands were padlocks, sealing a ghostly figure from view.

Malachi walked round the apple-tree.

"You can tell me to go, Rosie. Rose."

"No. I need to understand. Let's," I gestured to the bench and we moved to sit down as he tried to take my hand again. My fingers were blue, as if terror had stopped the blood flow.

"You won't remember but I do. When I first came to Tushita, I knew you straight away. Rose. I said 'Rose' and took you by surprise. You didn't seem to know me at all but I guess that's testament to time; I lived it hard down in Wales, you know. So much went on. You know what I mean? And without the punk, a Rolex for a badge, it's no wonder you didn't know me. I kept quiet but the coincidence of finding you again in the commune, Tushita, stopped me short, even then. It was difficult, though. I didn't want them to get hold of the story about Lesley and the baby in the commune. They'd have torn me to shreds. I tried to tell you. In that hotel. Got it wrong. I was all muddled up by then. It pushed me over the edge though." I extended my hand, now nothing but a frozen, leaden conductor of grief, to take his and rest the two hands between us.

"And all this time; that was thirty, 1977, 26 years ago, Avalon. Malachi. And why the intrigue and the internet? Why the bloody hell couldn't you just say? We spent a night in that bloody van, for god's sake. We might as well have come here."

"Graham. The fat man? Wouldn't he? You've never written to me about him. And. . ."

"I've never written to you about anything. You are bloody unreliable Welsh bearded Tom, for Christ's sake. Don't start getting at me about infidelities."

"Feisty yet still my Rosie." The shaking resumed and the IKEA wrap leaked vaporous petroleum fumes from its plastic threads.

"Not so much of the 'my'. You're not going to go all crazy on me are you?" I took my hand away. "I'm not, you know? I'm not up for a re-run of radical therapy and commune life, you know? I've done nutters. Gavin finished that one for me good and proper, as you know, bearded Tom. And I'm afraid that, much as I loved our night in the van, the romance and the absurdity, I'm looking for something a bit more substantial you know? I'm through with watching grass growing by itself and waiting for Spring. And why? I just don't see why you couldn't just say. How do you explain that one?" The Brian Rix farce had fizzled out. I'd dumped two of the three suitors at once and the third, poor Graham, unceremoniously rejected at the door, might well have done but for the Dolly Parton. I scratched, the chill of being taken for a ride giving way to hives. "Just tell me, Avalon. Do I have to hire Columbo or are you going to try and explain?"

"There's nothing I can say. I found you on-line and I genuinely always use the name Tom on the net; I told you who I really am but I used a different name and gradually it got away with me and I didn't know how to stop. I was

212

frightened and it all went too far. I couldn't tell you who I was at Tushita and then somehow, all these years later, with the net, I needed you to know but I couldn't tell you I was me. I left it far too long. I meant to tell you in Glastonbury and I was definitely coming to Streatley, but - and then we had that special night in the van and I couldn't say a word, couldn't tell you Avalon was Malachi and now Tom that you thought was called Tim. I'd blown it by then so I decided, hung for a sheep as a lamb, to come along and face the music." The front door slammed.

"Mum? Mu-um? Ah, there you are. Who the? Sorry, I'm, I'm Freya, and you're?"

"Malachi. An old friend of your mum's."

"Freya. This is, um. Well, you know, um." I cringed.

"I thought you were meeting your stalker today Mum."

"Stalker?" he asked.

"You," I explained.

"Him?" asked Freya.

"Yes. I'll fill you in. Or perhaps you'd like to give your own account, um, Tom?" He blushed as Freya, raising her eyebrows and turning to grab a 'Milton Keynes City of Dreams' T-shirt from the washing line scoffed,

"Explain? Don't bother. I've got enough trouble with my own life without the bloody parents' lives getting in the way. Rob and I were thinking about getting net-nanny put back on the computer. I'll text him; he'll have to come back tonight after all. We can't tolerate this for much longer. Now. I just wanna know. Can I get that lift you promised earlier?"

"Yes. 7pm?"

"Ok. We'll talk in the car, not that I think it'll be quite a long enough journey. You'll be off soon, won't you Tom, or Mikey or whatever you're called? I don't know. The older generation. Bloody nightmare."

As the bathroom steamed up and Freya prepared for an ordinary night on the tiles, I wished I'd kept it simple at her age. Avalon, now Malachi but lately Tom, devolved the mysteries of his intricate web. I warmed but the cold, bitter perspiration of shock mediated to protect me from the sway of his tender touch and I kept my hands beneath the plastic throw. He filled in the gaps.

"After Tushita, that night in the group room with that bastard Simon and all the drama bullshit, I tried to get away. I spent that first night in a ditch somewhere between the commune and the Bannisters' house next door and I walked into Wallingford the next day, finally catching six buses and finding my way back to Wales. I've been based there ever since. A friend of Slash's got me into the local psychiatric place when I turned up in there, shaking, where I got some help. It was the first time I'd really talked about Lesley and the baby – never even mentioned it in a group. It gave me some relief but I also got mixed up in all that Punk stuff again with Slash; drinking myself to a stew. I had never meant to leave Wales in the first place; Vamoosh found me at a Vibrators' gig and with Slash's help, the two of them like, trapped me into going to the Last Chance Foundation for drug addicted personalities in 1974. They told me it was a party so when I rolled up with a few lines of this and that the last thing I was expecting was a 48 hour encounter marathon. I thought I'd died and gone to hell. Not much changed, really, between then and when we met again in Tushita. I'd been off the drugs for three years, sure, but I was well and truly screwed up and nothing much was different except my outfits and being called a therapist; like a younger and more orange Gavin, I suppose. Took you in for a while, I suppose. I'm sorry Rosie love."

"Go on."

"Floundering I was and launched onto the group scene, running encounter groups in Pune and London; had no fucking idea what I was doing."

The phone called me away. Sarah wanted an update and I told her he scored neither a 10 nor a 1, although he might have earned both awards had things been different. She said she'd come round for the detail but I didn't see her for days since she and Dave had such a big bust up that afternoon that she hit the Cointreau a bit too hard and had to go into hospital for a few days to be fed *Resolve* intravenously. On my return to Tom-cum-Avalon-cum-Malachi's review of the group scene on the garden bench, he told me he'd decided that it wasn't all bad.

"It doesn't bear thinking about now, not for long. There are people, though, who say that whole group thing saved their lives, despite the fact that the therapists were mostly nutters who ruined their own." We looked at the carelessly thrown Greek salad with posh white bread in preference, we agreed, to the stoically healthy wholemeal of 1977. I asked him, as he declined a Stella and while we decided whether I would let him stay for lunch,

"Would you have had a Carlsberg? I can't remember. Does Tom still drink because I know for sure Avalon/Malachi does? We had the night in the barn. Oh yes. I was forgetting. They're all you. But seriously. Addictions. What do you do?"

"I still have a drink, now and then, but I shouldn't. Not really. I didn't think I was an alcoholic. I just stopped. Well, I say 'just' but both the circumstances and the withdrawals, the habits after that, it was all hell. I can't trust myself with anything; chewing biros could probably become a compulsion. Do you know what I mean?"

"I'm afraid to admit it but yes I do know what you

mean. Only too well." I'm not sure he had really wanted an answer. He was determined to tell me his story.

"No. It was my Dad, I think. His drinking. I went home one day, took the bus to Northampton just to see how things were, do you know what I mean? I planned to keep my head down fairly low, you know, of course and it was fairly traumatic going back there in the first place. I only used to go to my bench for my Lesley visits. But going back to the house was something I avoided at all costs. But I went one day. Haven't you had enough? I thought you'd be furious with me."

"I am but I'm also extremely nosey. But I, well. I just don't understand."

"Anyway, Dad had fallen over, in the night. He'd got up in a stupor and tried to get to the toilet. That's what I think. He'd got his trousers undone and opened a drawer in a dresser. I don't know why men do that. You know? They lift the lid of something; you wouldn't catch a woman raising the seat of a dining room chair."

"Luminosah did that. Don't you remember the famous story? He couldn't figure out why his parents weren't speaking to him. They were chilly. Because. He was well known for this. He'd been out and got absolutely off his face. All warm beer and not enough pickled eggs or cheese and onion crisps to sop it up. Then he took himself off to bed until he felt the need for a pee. Being a sensible sort, he found the right place: lifted the lid; finished; lowered the lid; turned off the light and went back to bed. The only problem was, you know those stereograms they had in the 70s? A turntable in the middle and lots of shiny Formica pretending to be mahogany with a speaker on either side? He'd left his parents sitting in the lounge with the telly on and the light off."

"Luminosah. Was he the really tall one? Yes. I can, no.

Well." Warming, I tried to help him out.

"Sorry. It doesn't matter about Luminosah. Your dad. It's not so bad."

"No. Well, you know. That's not it. I'm sorry. No. Well, you know. Poor man. He'd fallen, with the drawer open and his willy hanging out, you know. Hit his head on the corner of a Welsh dresser in Northampton, not Wales. Ha! and died in the night all alone." Malachi Tom had found the funny side.

"You found him? Your Mum?"

"I did. Yes. Mum? Died the year before. Heart. She wasn't living there by then. Was in Wales, near me and the kids. No. I did. I found him. On his own. I did. And that was it really.

I had the two kids by then. I thought, 'enough's enough' and my wife, she was well gone by then. She, well, good thing she went, well, you know, more horror stories if you want them. She lived, my daughter goes to see her, she comes to hassle me sometimes, steal my van, eat my food but it's an empty life. It's because we're getting on. I'm sorry."

"How sad. Funny that. When I first met Gavin, he had his kids. Different reasons but it's odd. The therapist thing. Perhaps you should have been allowed to develop mothering skills and be damned with the neurotic world. No wonder you had a breakdown. Grief. So young."

"We've all had a life, Rosie. Stuff happens. We have to get on somehow. You were full of nothing when I met a rosy Rose, that day in Streatley. Full of generosity and innocent confidence and I've wanted to." He slipped £5 across the table and I put it, silently and unacknowledged, in my pocket.

"If only."

It was civilised in the circumstances and Freya need not have worried about the menopausal smut. Leaving, as he turned on the door-step to look back through the house we had just walked through towards the garden beyond, we touched cheek on cheek uneasily. I said,

"Well, there's one thing. I never liked the look of welsh bearded Tom, anyway."

"Lead singer of Led Zeppelin. Didn't you know?" The spare can rattled in the back of his 'Sound Events' van as he disappeared again. Upstairs, to the side of the sink in the bathroom, he'd left the Rolex.

Blearily making my way to work the next day, I noticed the Wedgwood platter, still waiting to be returned to its place on the shelf after its outing to the reunion just two days before. There it remained, shoved onto the back seat of the car between two pairs of Tesco's stretch-jeans I'd bought, on special offer, shopping for the cream for the puddings, and I worried; I had thought myself, once, part of a revolutionary elite and yet now my taste was just that of the many, and I couldn't decide whether my enjoyment of Tesco's clothes was the effect of a coincidence of style and taste or social engineering. One thing I did know, though, was that I would be happy to be home without Premda, Jan, Malachi/Avalon or any other spectres from long ago, to make friends with ordinary life once again.

I dawdled on my way home from work, stopping at a vegetable stall and the garden centre, arriving home at dusk. As I pushed my own front-door open the Rolex told me I was late and I thought I had slipped into a parallel existence as a waft of Premda's fish-stew hit me full in the face.

"Darling. Where have you been? Jan and I got here ages ago."

"Sorry, Premda. I'm. I'm a bit, um. I thought you were staying over at Jan's."

"Yeah, my love. Bit of a change of plan. We decided to come over to yours."

"Oh. Lovely. When you say, 'we'?"

"Me and Jan."

"You, Premda. Premda and Jan."

"Yeah. Mmmmm. Come on, give me a hug." Premda laid the joint he was smoking in a hand-painted rice bowl of Japanese origin, inherited from my grandfather in 1985, dropped the stirring spoon into the depths of his fish-stew on my stove and grabbed me, crooning in my ear, "yeah. Mmmmm. Yeah, Yesser. Yeah. Jan's son, you know, Daniel? He's 35, yeah? Yeah, Daniel, he didn't really take too kindly to me shagging mummy. I thought differently, you know? How many more chances has she got? I thought I'd give her something she really wanted for her 70th, you know?" Premda had been in Australia long enough for me to forgive the upward intonation of his sentences and I, resorting to Englishness, moved to his right, smiled and nodded.

Jan was in my bath. Freya and Rob had left a note.

Gone to The Booths' House.
Ring Freya's mobile.
Where the fuck are you?
Rob and Freya.
(REMEMBER US? We're your kids, remember?)

Jan, in my new fluffy dressing gown, an advance birthday present from the girls at Aerobics, and some cosy socks I kept hidden under my pillow, beamed.

"Rosie. Lovely Rosie. We knew *you'd* understand, only, Daniel, poor Dan, he's terribly protective. I'd told him I'd gone to lie down, this morning, Monday – I knew Dan had to go to work and the poor lad, he was looking for my car keys. He just couldn't handle it. He came in to the bedroom, looking for the keys and, well. Premda and I were doing some terribly naughty things. He just, Daniel, he just blew."

"What? What? I mean, what did he do?"

"Oh, Niyati. Poppy, sorry. Rosie. He just went mad. He accused Premda of taking advantage of me. Me! He told Premda he had to 'Fuck off out of *my* house' the damn cheek of it. *My* house. I'm 70 years old and he just cannot understand I'm a woman. And my God, do I feel like a woman today."

"Alright. Stop. Ok. Jan. Brilliant. And, um."

"So, darling Poppy. Sorry, Niyat, sorry, Rosie. Can we stay here for a little while? Few days? I am going to take Premda to the Cotswolds. I've waited 20 years for this."

"22, isn't it? 27 since you met?"

"Oh, Rosie. You're *so* pedantic, darling. Let's all have some of Premda's fabulous fish stew."

Later, in the dead of night, my kids suffering behind bolted bedroom doors, a screech and the rebounding mattress springs were the only warning the cold night offered before Premda's congratulatory roar.

"Oh Jan. Jan. I - love - your - great - big – cunt."

It was a work night.

In the morning, Rob, a recent convert to the world of employment with a job in leisure management, said,

"Pick up some milk? Find myself some lunch? You're joking aren't you? Today? I'm telling you Mum. They've got to go. Mum. Get rid of them and I'll unlock the computer for you. Take the password off. But not until."

"Ok. Fair enough. Seems reasonable. Sorry. Yes, my lovely. Yes. I know. I'm sorry, while you're under such pressure." Scrabbling, I found Tom's fiver in my pocket. "Look, here's. Have a special lunch today. Yes?"

I turned, heaving the burnt fish-pan into a cardboard box, which I hurled through the back door narrowly missing Premda who surprised me, shaking the last drops of piss into my struggling Californian Lilac.

"Hey, Hey. Niyati."

"Rosie, Premda. Rosie."

"Not something you can really give up is it? Sannyas. Seeking. Bhagwan."

"Oh Premda. I'm trying. That's all. Trying. I quite like it, you know, ordinary life."

"Dahr-ling. Mmmm. You want to have a bath with me?"

"Fuck off Premda. Just fuck off." He laughed his head off.

Two days later, they left, handing me a letter the postman had tried to push into Premda's navel as the door swung open by surprise. Premda called,

"Big love, Niyati," as he and Jan disappeared to an anonymous hotel, where time and space made quite a big hole in Jan's credit card.

I read the letter. It seemed longer than three days since the compote for lunch.

Dear Rosie.

Thank you. I was expecting a tirade but you were kind and understanding. Thank you. I know it was wrong. You'll never forgive me, will you? I am sorry. Especially for the fright; and the driving. Streatley really wasn't my fault. Slash got in a mood, nicked my keys and took off leaving me stranded. It was true, though, about Glastonbury. It was the anniversary and I have tried to get to Northampton every year. But that's it now. 30 years of revisiting a spot. Time. It's been a struggle, all along, reclaiming the past.

It's just been me and the kids since Slash left me to take care of them in 1982. Not that I've lived a celibate life; the usual mix of disastrous experiments, like yours probably, don't need much discussion. But they saved my life, really, the kids. I had something to do being dad but when she left, and all through the long years, I wondered where you'd gone. I didn't dare get in touch with the others - the crazy mob - Premda and his friends - not even to try and locate my Bang and Olufsen stereo which I've always regretted leaving in the commune - and it was genuinely only by chance that I found a photo of you in the crowd; it was on the net, advertising the annual week long musical festival, when I was looking for gigs to support, so I came and I saw you in that pub where you danced. I know the area just a bit since my brother still lives in Silverstone, so he puts me up now and then. You changed your picture, so once you'd used it on the web yourself there was no room for misunderstandings – except from your side, of course, and I'm sorry that I didn't have the nerve to tell you then, that I was writing to you, Tom like. That Avalon who was Malachi was Tom too. What a mess. And Tim.

I don't know what you'll do with the watch. I've sometimes wondered if it's cursed but I wouldn't have left it if I still thought that. If it hadn't been for that particular crazy stuff, Vamoosh and the therapy bullshit, I could well have suffered a worse and more dreadful fate. I hope it brings you luck, or £500!

Thank you for the lunch, despite everything, and the raspberries in that mush. Did you call it compost? That can't be right. The chocolate cake was great. Your cooking's got a lot better since our commune days.

I'm 50 next year and I'm determined to be cruising in the new van along the southwest coast of Portugal for the summer. A friend of a friend mentioned something about a soul festival.

Love always.

Malachi. X

It was plausible.

2003

VIII

There was a frenzy of activity following the reunion, hot on the tails as it was of Jan's second husband's funeral, as she evacuated an ancestral home in the leafy lanes of the royal county. Auctions and transfers of pets complete, Jan finally ditched her twin-sets and pearls for the longed for life of radical therapy, colonic irrigation and experimental psychology in a sustainable-wooden building, South West Australia, arriving on Christmas Eve, 2003. With Premda. Much as Premda assured Jan she would die in his arms, he sustained an interest in, and conducted experiential research into, cunts of all shapes, sizes and ages, insisting nothing should inhibit his giving and sharing of love.

I lurked, the following year and the next one, in dark corners of the music festival that I might hear word and if it came at all it was in the plaintive soul singer Kevin's tribute to "Key" (Malachi to his mum), his roadie and his friend. Kevin's song, in the style of David Gray, was a catalogue of grief:

Key, Mala-key-key-key, soul-brother of his, got the rights to his song after the previous year's long hot summer supporting the fringe-soul-brigade, jumping on the band-wagon of a heavy-rock festival. He was a soulful man, dark secrets deep inside. On tour, gazing into the stars, Key Key Malachi confided his fears, over a few beers; money was short but he had one burning dream to pursue; he'd promised his girl Rosie he'd be home, he just had this one thing to do to.

The chorus of the song saw this quest as a treacherous-rite-of-passage that only a love-troth could presage, but hardened hostelry heart-breakers suppressed a titter as the story drew to a close. Our hero, poor Malachi, Key, Key, Key, who faced a tenacious fear of bungee, bungee, gee, gee jumping, had resolved, at the end of the summer-long-heavy-soul-bonanza-ode, to pay his way, face the day, on his half a century and then go home and propose. More Country than Soul, Malachi's fate was sealed when the broken-band of his one and only bungee-gee-gee-jump, ever, plunged him head-first into rocks just beneath shallow blue Atlantic waters on the far south-west coast of Portugal.

I would still gaze, for a year or a decade perhaps, across the fields, from the house with its cavernous views, imagining Avalon-Malachi's van, twisting through the lanes towards me and taste the bitter-sweet adrenaline of dreadful joy that he'd appear once more.

Jan emails: Rosie, darling. You must come and see my fabulous lemon trees.

I reply: Can't, lovely Jan. Addicted to drizzle, don't you know?

2005

I stood in an expanse of cotton-mixed fabric: vest tops in stripes and piles of denim low- rise combats, amidst the hungry bargain hunters swelled with slayers'pride, clutching my net-hooped bag bulging with a coat, four shoes and a string of beads. To my right, a towering display of bangles, silvered glass, caught my heart and I saw the face of the woman in Pune as she folded my small, young, plump hand into a cylindrical receptacle for dancing rows of shiny splendour.

At Christmas, a passing spirit brought beautiful silk-scarves from Cambodia, Thai Silk; one for Freya in stripes, one for Gran in powder-blue and another, spice-red for me. I wondered at the co-incidence of this lovely girls' dressing of me, a quarter of a century on, in the colour of the rising sun. And sunset.

2009

I was pottering in July, working on the latest exhibition of local and visiting artists' work. Community Arts anticipated its demise as a new star, Thatcher-like, rose on the horizon. Making hay, the artists' theme-cum-tag-line for the summer's exhibition was 'symbiosis' which was, I thought, incredibly corny but it was all about encouraging people to be mutually supportive and getting co-operatives together. They had decided to call it a symposium rather than an exhibition and I kept calling it the wrong thing. It was my old linguistic disability again; or should that be 'the linguistic' rather than 'my'? I was never quite certain whether I had got the disability or it had got me. The point was that you just looked at an exhibition but you could truly get inside the workings of a symposium. It seemed like a good enough ideal and in mid-life, while the kids both seemed more or less stable, old git behaviour filled a gap, especially since I got paid for thinking of it.

I liked the advisory and interactive parts of community arts admin but the evaluations, SMART targets and spreadsheets were a pain. I had taken to sneaking off early from the studios' office to live a whole day again in the summer afternoon sun. Potting on, having sold the Rolex and invested instead in a plastic greenhouse from *In-store* at the bargain price of £69.99, I was interrupted when a woman, recently arrived in the village, walked up the garden path. I had been there long enough by then but she'd only done her first six months and felt very much on probation with the village committee. She wanted to draw me in.

"I feel like I've stepped into some kind of Bohemian world here," showing me she'd found out who I was.

"Oh I don't know. I think this place is a bit too posh for us. It's worrying. My purple door, messing up the symmetry. And when I forget to bring the bins in."

"Well, you know, we could almost be in the middle of the wilderness here. It's brilliantly quiet but not quite as benevolent as you might think. Up the road, there. Have you seen them? The red kites, circling?"

"No. I. I'd love to, although, they used to be rare but now they're a pest."

"Like single-parents and aroma therapy," illustrated the neighbour, revealing her eligibility for membership of the village committee. "Oh dear, I didn't mean. I'm terribly sorry. We'll have to get together, do a spot of twitching but I can't stop now. I've brought this parcel. Misdirected. The postman left it, sorry. I've had it for a couple of days and it must have taken a while. From Australia."

"Ah! It's from Premda. A nutter. Nothing that can't wait, I'm sure. Thank you." The new neighbour sped away.

The package was decorated on the outside in felt-tip patterns with gold and silver permanent pen in swirls and curls. The address was difficult to read but the name 'Rosie', supported by a visual aid in the form of a big pink blob and a jagged stick, stood out. I carefully, yet still with a rip, teased up a glued end and folded the packaging flat.

Premda had had an idea. There was a note and pass the parcel like, another package inside wrapped in orange silk with silver stars.

Beloved Niyati.
Love.
Jan and I were talking this evening, watching the sun go down and feeling powerfully to connect with you. I want to share a time/space/free communion across this distance in an experiment. Since the reunion, I have been feeling that, more and more, the illusion of time and space is all that separates us.

I am feeling to share some ecstatic adventures we have just returned from, with the Shamans up in the hills. They have an inspired creative enlightenment project to share and I'm sending you a gift.
Open the package, Alice.
Big Love.
Premda.

Inside the starry silk, there was an A5 glossy advertisement, wrapped and tied with cotton around a small brown-paper, stapled, packet of something light, soft and lumpy. The advertisement provided what appeared to be the only clue. It was for 'ice', a programme of expressive arts events. This must be Premda's inspired creative enlightenment project. Further information could be obtained from Patrick Connor at www.ice.com.

Something happened, like the phone, and I pushed Premda's presents to the end of the kitchen table and beneath a newspaper. Sarah arrived. She had had to join the world of work having finally ditched terminally un-shaggable Dave and, after a long week away training Thompson tour operators, she had one night only to cash in on the opportunity to plan a summer of dancing in the sun, as schedules and diaries ate into her. I'd offered her supper, her integrated hob and tumble drier now a thing of the past. My home gaped. I seemed to spend my life trying to fill it up or get away; from time to time Rob or Freya would come home only to leave again and I didn't object if Sarah wanted to give away tacky sunshine vouchers for a bit of a reprieve from daily life.

As Sarah organised the summer, I was barely present, ticking off passages on a planner as I was silently and obsessively preoccupied with Premda's silvery orange parcel. Sarah passed out and stayed the night on the settle next to the kitchen table, close beside the parcel. Upstairs, I slept a shallow sleep, turning half-hourly, checking the steady green glow of the figures on the digital alarm.

Sarah, dashing out early next morning, left a note scrawled on the inner side of the postal package that had contained Premda's presents.

Sorry am such a pisshead. Have taken eggs and cheese as you insisted but thanks for the mini shitakes. I left you half of everything. Saves thinking. We can each have a mushroom omelette tonight. I'll ring but see you in Ibizia. Stay out of trouble. Laters. S x

I waited for the click of the back-door closing. I had decided. I'd turn the computer on then put the kettle on. Once I'd got some coffee, I'd be ready to find Patrick Connor's web address and get a few answers. Light flooded the room as I peeled back the curtains across the window to the east and I moved towards the end of the kitchen to turn the computer on. There on the table was the note. I recognised the paper, panicked and didn't read the note. I spun to find the outer-package and the newspaper missing from the other end of the table, as were its contents and I spun again to pick up the note on the torn package. A remnant of a plan made me move to the other end of the kitchen and flick on a switch to boil the kettle. I paused, leaning against the kitchen sideboard, and read the note. I read it again. Shitake. Mini shitake. Mushrooms? I think I liked it better when Sarah was still having phone sex with Dave, 'Harry met Sally' like, as she pored over a chip-butty, making faces at me on the comfortable end of her sofa while he tried to get her to take him back. Somehow she had managed to lose the house but climb a social class.

I was mesmerised by the trouble Premda had taken over colouring in the design of his envelope although a minute ladybird had been initialled 'J' and I thought that perhaps Jan had done all the hard graft. The kettle clicked off and I absently filled the waiting pink cup behind me on the counter where I leaned with my back to it. It looked a bit insipid so I added a spoon of Nescafe and moved to put the cup next to the computer. There on the floor as the chair scuffed, I found the advertisement for 'ice' with contact details for Patrick Connor and his website 'ice dot com'. Just beyond the crumpled ad., sliding under the leg of the table, was a strip of orange silk with silvery stars but the lumpy brown paper parcel had disappeared.

I got straight into ice dot com and gasped at the smiling face of Patrick Connor as a catalogue of his life and artistic achievements played out before me, in a moving slide show of its intersections with my own life.

Transfixed I stared at the screen, sipping the insipid foul coffee mixture absently as it cooked to a crunchy slime that slurped down the sides of the cup as the last of its half pint trickled away with the ticking half hour. Patrick's video began in 1972 with a sequence of shots of my father's compost heap, its shape transformed through a gradual sculpting of its form into a rough hewn fairy bed. It seemed the sculptor must have worked through the seasons to frame the photographs with twining creepers and heavy early apples growing from blossom. Finally, when he felt the ground mossy enough and the sculpted debris fit, he welcomed his guest as if he were Oberon and she Titania. Fairies tended desires. As Patrick's story unfurled, it became mine. He had taken a photograph of himself there, beside the perpetual decay of garden waste, annually between 1974 and 2009. In the first of the sequence, he stood within an infant rose arbour, tiny trees reaching upwards to grow into an arc of coppiced hazel, framing the entrance to the over-world. Each year's photograph moved across the screen and I saw Patrick ageing, almost imperceptibly at first, as a rose-arch grew rapidly and then, entering the fourth decade, his hair turned as roses linked arms across the eternal distance and became stronger and more vigorous than he.

The computer whirred and strained against the morning, billowing out vibrations, as the photographs gave way to video sequences shot all over the world of Patrick Connor's imposing bronze installations. Back tracking music that perfectly mimicked the memory as it was thrown onto the screen before me beat time. In 'Meditate' he had created an amber mass of swirling limbs, locked in a forced embrace with contorted smiles, seen from above in a white walled cube through a clear, glass ceiling. I shivered against the horrors of the rat pack encounter groups of the 1970s. This was the first of a series cut from sharp brass, some embedded with thick mottled glass, encased in white cubes. The second, 'Camelot', depicted a body hanging by its feet from a coiled rope of twisted sinews of fraying brass threads. Bob Seger implored, 'why don't you stay?' Behind the figure, four vast windows had been blacked out, panes replaced with brass cushions, spikes of copper worming from their seams like horse-hair from an ancient bed. Just one crack in the windows' blank stares permitted a glimpse, beyond, of vivid blue Atlantic coastal sky falling into the waves breaking onto jutting rocks below.

The third box, 'Love', contained a cross section revealing an unborn child, holding its hands against the glass front of its womb which carried the shadow of a tarnished steel-capped boot, breaking through the glass. Beyond, a staircase led to the glass-ceiling through which the scene was viewed and here, on the third stair from the bottom, sat a woman, bent over the protruding limbs of another, older child, his knees scuffed, her hands contorted with arthritic pain. 'Devotion' showed a syrup of dissolving bronze as dancers disintegrated and puddled round the feet of an empty chair from which a spherical light turned disco-glitter to fall, confetti-like, against the tight white boundaries of the box. Doves turned to split, dark pistols weaving bullets through the brilliant fragments of coloured light.

In the final installation, 'Brazil', stood a wizard centre stage in a heavily decorated pagoda. There were branches woven into the eaves of its roof to hold up heavy, curved, tiles of polished bronze glittering in the sunlight; bending close the camera showed not wood but finely carved and acutely observed bodies, bowing under the strain of holding the illusion together. I cried. I looked again as the wizard

232

drew me in; peering closely I saw myself. The wizard's face was mine. Or it could have been that mine was hers. Inside, suddenly, dancers lost in bodies moved as if alive, to grow wings made from the curving bronze tiles transforming at a stroke to nothing but the rays of a too strong sun turning feathers to gold over a dark green sea.

The screen dimmed and soft lilting music soared, with the modal twangs of the east breaking through a soulful Marvin Gaye backing, as I moved across the room, absentmindedly topping up the dregs of the coffee concoction with warm water. A new soundtrack, underpinned by an 80s' dance-track, explained.

All over the world, people feel bound by time and space. Inspired Community Enterprise (ice) is the company and trading name of Patrick Connor, an international community artist who works with groups of people to help them commission works of art which communicate their experience of being in the world.

Commissioning agents are invited to email or telephone Patrick Connor to discuss local community needs.

As I peered into my coffee cup the phone rang.

"Hey Niyati. Big love, yeah. Mmmm. Did you get the mushrooms? I have no respect for the law, you know, yeah, mmm. But, I was saying to Jan. Jan was saying. Yeah. She's so. Yeah. It's a small place. Village. Small minds. We wouldn't want you to be getting trouble." Premda. I must have made a noise. "Yes. Mmmmm. Yes. Mmmmm. It's nothing to be afraid of now. Just drop a little water into a coffee cup. Add the shroomies and you'll be up there with the Shamans before you can say, 'fuck. I'm enlightened'."

"I think, um, I think."

"No, no, Niyati."

"Rosie."

"Rosie. Sorry. Love. No. Don't think about it. Don't think Niyati. Baby. Yeah. Love. Just. Hey. Big love, yeah. Pop the mushrooms in a cup; drink it like a cup of tea. Bob's your uncle." He laughed.

"What about the sculptor? The bit of paper?" There was some shuffling.

"Jan. She's going on about some fucking sculptor. Jan? Jan?" There was some more dance music from the computer as I swayed and then the whole show began again as Jan tried to explain that she had found the leaflet at some trade fair for artists that she'd been to and she seemed to remember that she used to have someone called Patrick, who was a sculptor, to help her out in the garden when she'd had her big house.

"In Pangbourne. Near Streatley. It must be twenty years, though, since I last saw him. He looks the same on the web, more or less. Good looking chap," she said. "I thought I'd shove it in, the flyer, since Premda was writing. See if he, Patrick, rang any bells."

"Ah." The morning was particularly splendid and the light shining through the kitchen in the gathering day, from east, south-east to west, shone through the glass-speckled candle holders lined up on the windowsill, setting the kitchen alight with fireworks.

"But anyway," went on Jan. "We took ours about five minutes ago. What about you? You only need about half the packet."

"Ah. Oh god, Jan. I wish you could see this."

"I can, my darling. I can."

I let the slide show punctuate the day. I worked out it took about an hour to run its course. Then it would start again. It was soothing and it helped me to think. I moved a deck-chair into the kitchen and swivelled to follow the light as it moved round the three walls, the three windows, and it felt as if I could be wearing a cork-rimmed sunhat on my head while watching the donkeys at Weymouth. I sent Sarah a text. Bugger it. She wanted an adventure.

Enjoy your omelette. R. x

She replied,

Will do. Your shitakes are in the pink-seaside mug. XX S

And I wrote,

Got it. Thanks. Will phone. R. x

I wasn't sure I'd dare.

As the day stretched on, the bright evening of midsummer drew me out into the garden to sit in the middle of the overflowing flowerbeds, a mixture of summer and spring debris, and I tried to still my breath to hear the skylarks, far too late in the day. Instead, the busy flutter of the blackbird and its nest.

I rang Sarah, lying on my back watching the light change high above and a high-summer moon, too impatient to wait for night, long after her mushroom omelette.

"Sarah?"

"I'm sorry. Funny evening."

"Sarah? What's going on?"

"Keep your hair on Marvin. Oh no, he's dead. His dad did it. We've got to find a way. Is John Martyn still alive?"

"Um."

"I don't wanna hear 'bout evil, only wanna know about love."

I rang the number on the website. He said,

"At last. I wondered when you'd call."

"Ah. Patrick. Hello. I'm calling on behalf of CHARTS (charity art symposiums) and, oh well. I think I may know you anyway. And I was wondering if you could, if you would, if you will come and take part in the Symposium for local and international artists in the area, my area, my village as it happens, in August?"

"Hello. How are you Rosie?"

"How did you know?"

"Premda. He rang me. Said he was with Jan. I remember Jan. She had an absolutely glorious garden down there by the river. I wish she'd phoned herself but anyway, now. She'd said, she told her friend, this Premda character, that she knew you. So he rang me because of the symposium but he needn't have really. Never heard of the guy. And somehow I knew or rather I hoped that if an English lady phoned, like you, it would be you. And so it is, so."

"Do you think, it's short notice, this August."

"I would love to see you, Rosie."

"No. Yes. But. The CHARTS symposium? It's called 'Symbiosis' I'm afraid."

"I'll be there anyway. Doing some work with the refuge. But will you do me a turn, Rosie Sweet Rosie?"

"Yes."

"Meet me at the airport. Heathrow Terminal 4. August 1. It's a bit early, sorry. 5.20 am I'm afraid."

"Of course."

"Oh. And, I'll write, of course. Your email?" I told him. "But do you think you could find me somewhere to stay?"

"I think so. Yes. I'm sure."

I tried to eat, toast and my mother's marmalade. I'd really gone off it. Marmite hit the spot. I made some tea. It was hard to know what was real. I retraced my steps and looked back at the diary that Sarah and I had planned the night before. It told me that, as I had to open the Private View on August 15, she had decided to go on ahead and explore Lisbon leaving England on the 31 July. We'd agreed that she'd meet me at the airport there on August 16. I thought that was a long way from Ibiza but I was not very good at geography and I knew that it was possible that I hadn't been listening when I'd changed my mind. Landlady-like, I could be realistic, I calculated that Patrick Connor could have two weeks of bed and breakfast before being left to his own devices in a secluded English hamlet. It would suit us both; he could feed the cat. I felt, at the same time, like a plant that had been growing in the wrong soil, looking at the possibility of a transfer to Kew.

Patrick only sent one email, just to let me know that we would need the day free on August 1 because we had to pick up a huge container and arrange its transport. The space it was going to, a large plot at the village site, had been booked through the exhibitors' agency under 'Confidential: VIP 1 of 1'. Could I come in a taxi to meet him? He'd pay. And no nonsense about how much. That didn't matter. I was floored.

And he sent white roses.

It was balmy and thank god the taxi driver wasn't in the mood for a chat. It was so early that only one village curtain twitched as I left on August 1 for the 5.20am rendezvous, just fourteen days before the exhibition, or symposium rather, would open with a Private View on August 15. Even at that time of day, road-works can bugger things up and I arrived, breathless, dropping voile scarves and coins, grovelling for my glasses under the arrivals board, late. He was holding an A4 display which read, 'Rose' printed in Batik on silk, in deep maroons and pink, carefully stitched onto its cereal-box backing. I smiled. He shook my hand and I led him to the information desk to enquire about his cargo.

Waiting in the VIP area, there was tepid coffee and nerves. He smiled. I smiled. We had to rent a Hertz car and drive to St Albans. I drove and we signed for his latest sculpture, buried in a tanker, releasing it for immediate onward transportation and delivery to the site of the exhibition. It was called 'Utopia' he said and it would need a couple of weeks to bed in. The tanker driver, dragging the installation behind the cab, broke all the rules and let us sit beside him so he could tell us off for being a couple of tossers; "Sorry about the language, love, idealists you would understand but tossers says it like it is".

Utopia was home. Patrick explained it was his extended Tracey Emin statement and a tribute to his muse. He wanted to demonstrate what a space could be if it lived in empathy with the landscape and its people. It was an ideal home. A Utopia which inspired nothing but the best in people.

Unveiled, as the sides of the tanker were folded away, a vast fig-shaped bulb of glass and brass nestled in the earth. Inside there were secret zones where light, mirrored down through tubes, lit womblike pockets and there were broader spaces where long lengths of pale ash plank reached towards the countryside beyond glass walls. Simple foils, rotated by whim or will, allowed light to be dimmed and coloured to represent sensation. Beyond, as if expecting a relationship, rosemary bushes and lavender brushed against the ventilation shoots mirroring sight with scent.

Patrick moved into a spare room in my house; it was full of things. Three walls were a cacophony of family history, in powerful black and white photographs, covering every inch. The fourth wall, framing the window, was wallpapered in a 1930s' pink-rose twirl and here the bed leant under the window pointing its foot forward into the room. Patrick turned the bed through 180 degrees so that his feet pointed towards the window, letting his pillows fall from the headless end rather than holding them trapped between him and the wall forcing him to gaze at history. We moved carefully round the house at night.

But in the daytime people came in mini-buses from the women's refuge to spend some time in Utopia. I was on information and advice, catapulted into a new dimension in the arts' admin arena, talking all day and contacting a well-pool of advisers to support the women's successful transition through the refuge to a freer life. When everyone left, weary by 5pm, Patrick and I pottered about in Utopia messing it up a bit. In sympathy with Tracey Emin, it was ok to leave your orange peel on the floor and write abusive messages about people you wanted to shame on the mirrored glass. It was a living thing that we could wipe clean and abuse again until we were ready to plant some trees.

A fortnight passed like this. Utopia was a hit with the press at the Private View on August 15 and Patrick and I stayed, staring out at the deepening skies through brass and glass mottled panels, watching the harvest moon rise again flooding the sky with roses.

Scented with lavender and dousing our cocoon in pink rainbows, deep in an interior pocket of our glassy-metal nest, flickering rays displaced complimentary raspberry leaf-vein patterns creeping round my ankles. I quivered and joked about an eye-test when he told me I was beautiful. I'd promised I was a bit of a sex goddess but instead we talked long into the night and dissected the years, falling asleep in our confessional.

ORANGE
Cherry Coombe

Orange is available in paperback and as an ebook from
amazon.co.uk and amazon.com
Further details about editions and new work from the
same author is available at www.cherrycoombe.com

WHAT HAPPENS WHEN SOMEBODY DIES
Cherry Coombe
www.cherrycoombe.com
2011/2012 (Amazon)

A collection of dark, sad and intermittently hilarious
auto/biographical stories of bereavement.

ABOUT THE AUTHOR

CHERRY COOMBE was born in 1956. Under a Labour government she was allowed to study while her own children were still at school. She graduated with a first-class degree in English in 2004 and now lectures in English. There is nothing remarkable about Cherry Coombe. She has not won the X Factor, found a cure for cancer or managed to stop the spread of palm oil plantations. She lives in the countryside. Her grown-up children come and go.

Those who have read ORANGE ask about biography; people ask if Rosie and her friends live at a real address; if Rosie is Cherry. Perhaps the story has a stronger grasp if the idea has real legs. ORANGE is driven by anxiety, obsession, grief and shock. Its heroine is promiscuous and not very good in bed. An admission of auto/biography is unlikely. Cherry is more likely to suggest that she is every character in the book.

News and the latest reviews: www.cherrycoombe.com

Made in the USA
Charleston, SC
15 October 2011